Jackie French's writing career spans 10 years, 32 wombats, 80 books for kids and adults, seven languages, various awards, assorted 'Burke's Backyard' segments in a variety of disguises, radio shows, newspaper and magazine columns, theories of pest and weed ecology and 27 shredded back doormats. The doormats are the victims of the wombats, who require constant appeasement in the form of carrots, rolled oats and wombat nuts, which is one of the reasons for her prolific output: it pays the carrot bills.

Her critically acclaimed book *Hitler's Daughter* won the Children's Book Council Book of the Year Award for Younger Readers in 2000.

To find out more about Jackie's new books — and life with wombats in the valley — register for her monthly newsletter at **www.harpercollins.com.au/ jackiefrench**.

Books by Jackie French

Fiction

The Roo that Won the Melbourne Cup • Rain Stones
Walking the Boundaries • The Boy Who Had Wings
Somewhere Around the Corner
Annie's Pouch • Alien Games • The Secret Beach
Mermaids • Mind's Eye • A Wombat Named Bosco
Summerland • Beyond the Boundaries
The Warrior – the Story of a Wombat
The Book of Unicorns • Dancing with Ben Hall
Soldier on the Hill • Daughter of the Regiment
Stories to Eat with a Banana • Tajore Arkle
Hitler's Daughter • In the Blood • Missing You, Love Sara
Stories to Eat with a Watermelon • Lady Dance
Stories to Eat with a Blood Plum
How the Finnegans Saved the Ship
Dark Wind Blowing • A Story to Eat with a Mandarin
Ride the Wild Wind • Blood Moon • The White Ship
Phredde and the Leopard-skin Librarian

Non-fiction

How the Aliens from Alpha Centauri Invaded My
Maths Class and Turned Me
Into a Writer ...
How to Guzzle Your Garden • Book of Challenges
Stamp Stomp Womp & Other Interesting Ways to Kill Pests
Seasons of Content • The Best of Jackie French
Earthly Delights
The Fascinating History of Your Lunch
The Secret Life of Santa Claus

Visit Jackie's website
www.jackiefrench.com

A STORY TO EAT WITH A Mandarin

Phredde and the Temple of Gloom

JACKIE FRENCH

Angus&Robertson
An imprint of HarperCollins*Publishers*

Angus&Robertson
An imprint of HarperCollins*Publishers,* Australia

First published in Australia in 2001
Reprinted in 2002
by HarperCollins*Publishers* Pty Limited
ABN 36 009 913 517
A member of the HarperCollins*Publishers* (Australia) Pty Limited Group
www.harpercollins.com.au

HarperCollins*Publishers*
25 Ryde Road, Pymble, Sydney, NSW 2073, Australia
31 View Road, Glenfield, Auckland 10, New Zealand
77–85 Fulham Palace Road, London W6 8JB, United Kingdom
Hazelton Lanes, 55 Avenue Road, Suite 2900, Toronto, Ontario M5R 3L2
and 1995 Markham Road, Scarborough, Ontario M1B 5M8, Canada
10 East 53rd Street, New York NY 10022, USA

National Library of Australia Cataloguing-in-Publication data:

French, Jackie.
A story to eat with a mandarin: Phredde and the Temple of Gloom
For children 8 to 13 years old.
ISBN 0 207 19781 4.
I. Title.
A823.3

Cover, internal design and illustrations by Deborah Coombs
Printed and bound in Australia by Griffin Press on 79gsm Bulky Paperback White

9 8 7 6 5 4 3 2   02 03 04 05

To everyone in Dandenongs Pod,
Palmerston District Primary School
and the students in 3CR:

Alice	*Jesse M*
Kangandeep	*Luke*
Simon	*Joshua P*
Lauren	*Leilani*
Johnathan	*Ben*
Jessie D	*Leigh*
Tess	*Alexandra*
Natasha	*Emily*
James	*Jordan*
Jessica H	*Ganesh*
Richard	*Nicole*
Jack	*Jessica S*
Sam	*Jake*
Stacey	*Kevin*

and Chris Reeve and Barbara Braxton, who inspire them! Here is your dungeon, dark and slimy and with vampire bats, as you requested.

With much love,

Jackie

P.S. And to Jessica, because your best friend asked me to put you in this book!

Contents

Cast of characters

For those who came in late ...

Prudence

A normal schoolgirl who lives in a magic castle and has a fairy — sorry, phaery — as her best friend.

Phredde

A thirty-centimetre high phaery who likes pink and silver joggers and rock music. She hates phaery dances on the green and definitely does *not* want to marry a handsome prince when she grows up. Her real name is The Phaery Ethereal but it is *not* a good idea to mention this to Phredde.

Bruce

A handsome prince. Or he might be, if he hadn't decided to be a giant frog instead of a kid. (A *Crinea signifera*, if you want to be precise. Ask Bruce if you want to know more about *Crinea signifera* — or better still, look it up, because Bruce will tell you more than you want to know.)

Bruce admires frogs. He likes flies too (the fatter the better) and mosquito pizza. He's in Pru's and Phredde's class at school.

Bruce's Parents

Nice people — sorry, nice phaeries. They're quite tolerant of having a frog for a son, especially when he threatens to turn into a slug instead if they raise any objections.

The Phaery Queen

Well, she's a queen. And a phaery. What more need I say?

Mark

Pru's older brother. He's also a werewolf, a trait he inherited from his father's side of the family. Answers to 'Dog's Breath' — but don't try it if you can't run fast.

Pru's Dad

Loves everything South American, except possibly jaguars, piranhas, enormous boa constrictors and giant sloths.

Pru's Mum

Loves crosswords and coffee and is just beginning to understand computers. Fusses about the least little thing, like vampires, ogres and going out in the sun without a hat and sunblock.

Pru's Great Uncle Ron

Retired butcher. He is also a werewolf.

The Phaery Valiant

Phredde's dad. Prefers to be called Jim.

The Phaery Splendifera

Phredde's mum. Loves crosswords, honeydew nectar and racing magic carpets. Has *The Directory of Handsome Princes* on her bedside table.

Amelia

In Pru's, Phredde's and Bruce's class at school. Good at ... well, everything, according to Amelia. You don't really want to know anything more about her.

Newcomers ...

The Phaery Daffodil

Graduated top of her class in Evil Studies at Phaeryland University.

Mordred

Her son. He's studying Special Effects at technical college.

Prince Peanut

A *really* handsome prince. Also vegetarian.

Plus ...

731 vampire bats
2 trolls
24 giant, blood-sucking mosquitoes
3 little pigs (well, great fat hogs, actually)
1 bogeyman (sorry, bogeyperson)
a big bad wolf (a bit covered in yuk)
a soooo cute bunny rabbit
an invasion of flesh-eating ghouls
a plumber called Dwayne
and a special guest appearance by Snow White and the seven quite short computer software engineers ...

Prologue

(ie you have to read this bit first so it terrifies your toes off before you start the real story)

Lightning shuddered above the castle. Wind screamed through the dungeons as though someone had shoved red-hot nails up its fingernails — which is pretty impossible when you think about it, as wind doesn't have any fingers, and anyway, it was Tuesday, and the inhabitants of the Temple of Gloom only tortured their victims on Friday afternoons. (It made them taste nicer when they ate them for Saturday lunch.)

It was a dark and stormy night, too. It was *always* a dark and stormy night outside the Temple of Gloom. Vampire bats flapped around the turrets. Wolves howled into the night, and a tortured voice shrieked into the darkness.

'Will you turn that music down!'

The wolf howls lessened just a little.

'But Mum, it's The Werewolves' new CD!'

'I don't care if it's The Leaping Vampires ...'

'But Mum, *no-one* listens to them any more ...'

'Turn it DOWN! And get rid of those vampire bats too. They're giving me a headache.'

'But Mum, they're radio-controlled!'

'Radio-controlled vampire bats! What's wrong with *real* vampire bats?'

'They drip blood all over the place,' said the second voice sulkily. 'And they do their business on the sofa, too.'

'There are hundreds of perfectly good vampire bats down in the dungeon,' said the first voice. 'I don't see why you have to waste money on radio-controlled ones.'

'But Mum ...'

'How can I concentrate with howling wolves and radio-controlled vampire bats?'

'But Mum ...'

'Don't you see! She'll be here soon! The trap must be ready!'

'Oh,' said the second voice.

'I saw her in my magic mirror!' gloated the first voice. 'A delicious, tender, young human! Her name is Prudence. Just think what we can do with her! Prudence pie, Prudence pizza, Prudence pikelets with jam and cream ...'

'Oh ...' the first voice chortled evilly. 'It will be so good having a nice, young human for dinner again ...'

one

Just Another Day in the Castle

(ie the first chapter about people we already know — well, OK, people AND phaeries AND frogs — like Pru and Phredde and Bruce)

It was an ordinary day in our castle.

I was watching TV (it was this really cool kung fu movie) and Dad was feeding the piranhas (Did you know they can skeletonise a cow in ten minutes? And you should see what they do to a guinea pig!) and Mark was brushing his teeth for the eighty-fourth time that day, because my brother Mark turns into a werewolf every full moon, and gleaming white teeth are really essential for any teenage werewolf, and Mum was having a hissy fit all round the castle.

Mothers stress out at the least little thing sometimes, like their kids being captured by snot phaeries or chased by giant ogres.* Or, in this case, a simple family visit to Phaeryland.

'Shoes!' shrieked Mum, racing into the TV room just as the hero was about to kick ninety-six evil ninjas into oblivion. 'Prudence, what sort of shoes do they wear in Phaeryland?'

'Relax, Mum,' I said. 'They don't wear shoes, remember? Women wear glass slippers and men wear those really sexy black leather boots. Phredde's mum and dad'll take care of everything.'

'Glass slippers. Right,' muttered Mum. She dashed out of the room again just as the seventy-second evil ninja sailed into the ornamental pond.

Ten seconds and twenty-three evil ninjas later she was back again.

'My hair dryer!' she cried. 'Will I be able to plug in my hair dryer?'

'Mum, just calm down,' I said. 'You don't have to take a hair dryer into Phaeryland. You don't need to take *anything* into Phaeryland. It'll all be magicked up for you.'

Just for a second I wondered if I was right. I mean, maybe you did need a hair dryer in Phaeryland. After all, I'd only been there twice,** once by invitation to attend the Phaery Queen's birthday party, and the

*See *Stories to Eat with a Watermelon* and *Stories to Eat with a Blood Plum.*

**See *Stories to Eat with a Banana* and *Stories to Eat with a Watermelon.*

second time when Phredde and I sort of snuck in and got kidnapped by giant butterflies. But I haven't told Mum about that yet, so I'd appreciate it if you don't go mentioning it to her either.

I took a deep breath and turned off the TV, just as the final ninja fell into a barrel of water (funny how there's always a barrel of water around for evil ninjas to fall into).

Sometimes you really have to take a firm line with parents. 'Look, Mum,' I said. 'There's nothing to fuss about ...'

'Nothing to fuss about?' shrieked Mum. 'Just the Phaery Queen's wedding and we're all invited, that's all, and we're going to Phaeryland, and ...'

'It's Phredde's family who are really invited,' I pointed out. 'They just asked us to come, too. Mum, you don't have to worry about *anything* in Phaeryland! Phredde's mum will PING up everything we need, like glass slippers and tiaras and ...'

'Tiaras!' groaned Mum. 'I'll have to have my hair done! You ring the hairdresser — no, I'll ring the hairdresser — no ...'

'Mum, it'll all be taken care of,' I soothed. 'Just wait till Phredde and her family get here, and ...'

The door opened again and Dad marched in, wiping his bloody fingers on his jeans. (No, that is *not* a swear word. It's just that his fingers were messy. Piranha food can be a bit yuk.)

'Well, that's done,' said Dad happily. 'I've fed the piranhas, watered the rose garden, fed the unicorn, locked up the battlements, sealed the dungeons, raised the drawbridge, put fresh towels under the giant sloth ...'

'But Dad,' I said, 'no time passes when you're in Phaeryland. Not here, anyway. You just have to remember to ask Phredde's mum or dad to bring us back to the time when we left.'

'Better to be safe than sorry,' said Dad. 'Has your brother finished packing?'

'How should I know?' I muttered.

Mark was a sore point with me at the moment. Just because Mark was a werewolf — *and* older than me — he was getting to stay at Uncle Ron's, while I had to get all prettied up and go to Phaeryland.

Phaeryland!

Of course, if you've never been to Phaeryland you mightn't understand why I was upset. I mean, once you're too old to slop paint in a colouring book and spit your spaghetti out all over the floor you probably don't even think of Phaeryland from one moment to the next.

Phaeryland is *nice*. It's *just* like the pictures in those books — blue sky, green grass, phaery castles, big spotty toadstools and elf musicians playing that stuff we get in musical appreciation, *and* lacy dresses and *tiaras*, for Pete's sake. I mean, it's all so *cute* ... and here were my parents going all smiles and 'Whoopee!' about an invitation to stay in Phaeryland for a week and go to the Phaery Queen's wedding ...

Wedding. Huh! I bet she was getting hitched to

some poncy prince in tights and puffed sleeves and probably even a feather in his hat.

Well, you can see why I didn't want to go.

To be honest, there was something else as well. It's really hard to admit it because, after all, Phredde is my best friend, and Bruce is okay, too, I mean, sometimes I really like him, and I think maybe he really likes me too ... but at other times — well, you just can't help feeling jealous of people who can PING up just about whatever they want ...

... And, okay, phaery dances may be corny, but at least they're *interesting*. I mean, my family doesn't have *any* interesting habits at all, just Mum and her crosswords and Dad and his pet piranhas and Mark turning into a werewolf at full moon ...

BONG! BONG! BONG!

'That'll be the front doorbell,' said Mum. 'Just let the drawbridge down again would you, darling? I'll tell Gark to put the kettle on.'

Mum dashed down the corridor, down the stairs, down *another* flight of stairs and along another corridor to the kitchen, and Dad padded off down the stairs and through the Great Hall and out into the courtyard to let the drawbridge down. (Mum says that one day she'll remember to ask the Phaery Splendifera to put a few escalators in our castle, not to mention an automatic drawbridge.)

Soon there was a *flip, flip, flap* of wings outside the door and Phredde came fluttering in. Of course, given that Phredde's a phaery (and only about thirty centimetres high, although somehow you never notice that with Phredde), she could just have PINGED herself over here. But since Phredde's family moved here two years ago they've been trying to sort of fit in, which means getting the bus or driving around (even if it *is* on a magic carpet instead of in a Holden station wagon — but then again, they don't make phaery-sized Holden station wagons) instead of just going PING whenever they feel like it.

'Hi,' said Phredde glumly. Phredde hates Phaeryland even more than I do.

'Hi yourself,' I said.

Phredde flew over and perched on the arm of the sofa. She was still wearing her jeans, I noticed, just like me, except that mine were normal blue and Phredde's were bright turquoise with purple fringes.

'You ready to go?' I asked.

'I suppose,' said Phredde, even more glumly. 'At least this time you'll be there, too.'

'And Bruce,' I pointed out.

Phredde shrugged. The trouble with Bruce is that he's a phaery prince — well, he would be if he hadn't changed himself into a frog — and Phredde isn't too keen on phaery princes. Not when her mum keeps *The Directory of Handsome Princes* by her bed.

'Ethereal! Ethereal ... Oh, there you are!' Phredde's mum drifted into the room — forty centimetres of ball dress and tiny diamonds. 'It's time to get ready.'

'Mum, do I really have ...'

PING!

Suddenly Phredde's turquoise jeans, pink hair and purple T-shirt were transformed into a gold and pearl-encrusted ball dress, lace petticoats, tiara, glass slippers and long blonde hair.

'Mum!!'

I bit my tongue really hard to stop myself from grinning. 'Hey, Phredde, you look really ...'

PING!

And there I was — with a diamond-flowered tiara in my hair and my feet suffocating in these glass slippers and all this lace, and it was *pink*!

Phredde grinned. 'Now you look really ...'

'Don't say it!' I warned.

Tink, tink, tink down the corridor (I told you, glass slippers just aren't practical) and the door opened and there was Mum.

Well ...

My mum usually dresses okay for someone her age, mostly jeans or tracksuit pants, except once when she'd been up really late doing this big crossword with Phredde's mum and she came down to breakfast in jeans *and* tracksuit pants.

But I had never, *never* seen her look like this.

One dress, shaped a bit like an umbrella but wide enough to cover our classroom, just about, all in this red and gold brocade stuff — you know, like they put on chairs sometimes.

One tiara, with pearls the size of grapes and more pearls in her ears and sort of dangling down over her chest.

Glass slippers, and Phredde's mum must have PINGED her up a pedicure, too, because her toenails were bright pink through the glass. And lots and lots and *lots* of hair, sort of in Mum's colour but better, if you know what I mean.

She didn't look like Mum at all.

'Gloop,' I said.

Mum smiled, this really fuzzy, happy smile. 'Oh, Prudence, isn't it wonderful!' she breathed. She swirled round a couple of times, her long skirt sending a potted kentia palm flying.

'Yeah, fantastic, Mum,' I mumbled, setting the pot plant upright again. Well, you can't spoil parents' little pleasures, can you?

Then Dad walked in.

I'm not going to tell you what Dad was wearing. It's just too embarrassing. Well, okay, yes I am, because otherwise you won't know just how embarrassing it was.

Purple tights (I mean, they were *tight*; in fact, really rude if you must know) and a long red silk shirt with *ruffles*, for Pete's sake, and white lace at the wrists, a leather belt with rubies on it, these long leather boots (they were actually quite cool boots, even if the rest was dorky) and a red velvet hat with a feather.

'Hey, wow, Dad!' I said.

Dad stared at me. 'If you say one more word, Prudence ...' he threatened.

'I think you look lovely,' said Mum dreamily.

'Yeah, that's the word. Lovely,' I said, grinning.

'Prudence ...' began Dad, then he glanced at Mum. Mum hadn't looked so happy since the time she managed to get the cryptic crossword finished by dinner time.

'Yes, it's all lovely,' he agreed.

Then Phredde's dad, the Phaery Valiant (but he prefers to be called Jim) came in, and Phredde's mum made us all hold hands and I yelled out, 'See you, Dog's Breath!' to Mark.

And he yelled, 'See you, Prune Face,' to me. 'Take care!'

'There's no need to take care in Phaeryland,' I yelled back. 'Nothing can happen to you there!'

And Mum called out, 'Don't forget to ...'

But whatever advice she was going to give Mark for the 180th time, it was too late, because the Phaery Splendifera went PING.

And we were in Phaeryland.

two

Off to (Yuk) Phaeryland

There are two things you notice about Phaeryland.

The first is that it's nice — *really* nice — but I've already told you that. The sky was blue and the birds were singing, and I mean singing, like 'Tweet, tweet, tweet' instead of 'Caw, caw, caw' like the crows in the school ground that are after whatever they can snaffle of your lunch scraps and look like they wouldn't mind eating your eyeballs for dessert if you gave them half a chance.

And the second is that suddenly Phredde and the Phaery Splendifera and Jim were all the same size as us. (Phredde's explained that to me. It's all about the quantum fluctuations in the magic field which mean that in the real, ie non-magical, world they're diminished ... well, something like that anyway. Ask Phredde if you want to know any more, though to be honest, I don't think Phredde understands it either.)

Anyway, there we all were — Mum and Dad and me and the new super-economy size Phredde and her parents, with this green colouring-in-pencil-type grass and lollipop-like trees and a zillion flowers in red and blue and yellow all around our feet, blooming at us like they were planning to give us all hay fever, except I suppose you don't get hay fever in Phaeryland.

And just like the last time we were in Phaeryland, these great giant butterflies flip-flapped over the lollipop trees and landed beside us (I had to hold on to my tiara — you really get a draught from a giant butterfly), and we all climbed on and I realised I'd forgotten to take my car sickness tablets *again*, which meant the ride was really interesting for anyone underneath us, especially that elf sitting on his mushroom when I lost the muesli I'd had for breakfast. (It didn't look like muesli by then, of course, especially when it had fallen from 100 metres up.)

So the butterflies flapped, and I watched my breakfast sail down to become part of the ecology of Phaeryland, and Mum kept chirping things like, 'Oh, how wonderful! Oh, Splendifera, look at that castle ... and those cute little bunnies. Oh, is that a brook? Oh, Prudence, did you see those sweet elves dancing?'

'Gluuurrrp!' I said.

And then we landed.

I staggered off my butterfly thorax (we did insect anatomy in science last term) and Mum alighted like she was a princess or something, but not the kind who ride polo ponies or visit refugee camps. I mean, she was *graceful*, which isn't a word that usually describes Mum when she's just messing round our castle in her tracksuit. I gave a final burp, wiped my mouth and looked around.

We were in a forest glade (everything is in a forest glade in Phaeryland). There was a yellow brick road running through the trees and flowers that were all around us (naturally), and a little tinkling brook (I'm serious — it went tinkle, tinkle, tinkle like it was a mob of preschoolers practising for the end-of-term concert) with a cute little arched stone bridge over it, and this great pink and blue and yellow palace that looked like it was made of coloured icing sugar, all swirls and turrets, in front of us, with a sign over the front door saying 'Sweet Pea Guesthouse'.

There were lots of sweet peas about, too.

Phredde made a sort of vomiting noise behind me. (She was only pretending. Phredde doesn't get car sick — er, butterfly sick. I suppose it comes of all the flying she has to do.)

'Oh,' said Mum. 'Isn't it lovely? Look how those sweet flowers trail down from the window boxes, Prudence!'

Well, it was okay. It was big, anyway — I mean, it would have made a great meringue — but apart from that it, looked a bit like the sand castles I used to make at the beach before I got into fighting pirates and stuff like that instead.

So we climbed up a million steps (okay, forty-six) and into this great hall with carpets on the walls which Mum said were tapestries, and there, tapping at a computer behind a desk, was this really old guy, even shorter than me, with a red cap on his head and a long white beard and red cheeks.

'Hey,' I whispered to Phredde, 'that looks just like one of the gnomes in my picture book when I was small.'

'It *is* a gnome,' Phredde whispered back. 'You're in Phaeryland, dummy!'

The gnome looked up from the computer. 'Welcome to Sweet Pea Guesthouse!' he cried. 'I'm Mr Tiddlywinks. How can I help you?'

Phredde's dad strode forward. (He was dressed in really embarrassing tights and stuff too, but he looked like he was used to it. Well, resigned to it, anyway.) 'Reservations in the name of Valiant?' he said.

The gnome glanced at his computer. 'Ah, yes,' he said. 'Three doubles. I've put the kiddies in together.'

Kiddies! And I was taller than he was! Even Phredde was taller than him now!

But before I could say anything, or even kick him in the thorax, he was thumping his way up this great, wide staircase and Mum was looking so happy you'd think she'd start dribbling.

We got to our room eventually.

'Arrrk!' screamed Phredde as the door shut behind us. She kicked her glass slippers off so hard they bounced against the wall. I thought they'd break into a million shards, but they didn't. (I suppose glass slippers have to be made out of pretty tough glass.) So I just wriggled out of mine and let my toes breathe for a change and looked around the room.

Two four-poster beds with ruffly brocade stuff over them, one carpet with flowers on it (naturally), a big fancy mirror on the wall, and one small tinkling brook over by the window which I supposed was our bathroom (it had hot and cold taps on the wall above it).

I wandered over to the mirror.

'Mirror, mirror, on the wall,' I said, just for fun. 'Who is the fairest one of all?'

'Not you, chickie,' said the mirror. 'Your tiara is on crooked and you've got a spot of yuk on your ball dress.'

So much for magic mirrors.

'Oops,' I said. I wandered over to the tinkling brook and began to sponge the yuk off my ball dress. (It was only a tiny speck! A phaery on a speeding butterfly would never have noticed it.)

'Hey, Phredde?' I asked.

'Yeah, what?' Phredde was hauling the tiara out of her hair.

'If this stream is our bathroom, where do we, you know, go to the toilet?'

'We don't,' said Phredde.

'What! But I'll burst! You can't not go to the toilet for a whole week!'

'You can in Phaeryland,' said Phredde. 'They haven't even *heard* of constipation here.' She straggled over to the window, her train drooping behind her. 'Hey look, there's a rose bush!'

'So what?' I asked, peering out too. I mean, the whole place was just about dripping with roses.

'It means we can climb down the rose bush and escape for awhile,' explained Phredde patiently.

'But what about the thorns?'

'There are no rose thorns in ...'

'Yeah, yeah, I know, there are no rose thorns in Phaeryland. But won't our parents know we've gone?'

'We'll leave a note,' said Phredde. 'Anyway, they'll be fussing about their rooms and having cups of nectar for hours. You know what parents are like. And we'll be back for dinner.'

I glanced down at my ball dress. 'I don't know about you, but I don't think I *can* climb down a rose bush in this,' I admitted.

'Easily sorted,' said Phredde.

There was an almost silent PING! and I was wearing tracksuit pants and a T-shirt.

There was another PING and Phredde was out of her ball dress, too.

'Er, Phredde,' I said.

'Yeah?' asked Phredde happily, straightening her purple and silver T-shirt.

'You remember the last time we came to Phaeryland without ball dresses on? How we were kidnapped by giant butterflies because they thought we were caterpillars in our tracksuits?'

'No worries,' said Phredde. One more PING and we were both wearing baseball caps that had 'I am not a caterpillar!' written on them.

That seemed to sort that out.

So I opened the window, letting in all the flower power air and tweet tweet bird songs, and grabbed hold of the rose bush and jumped off the balcony and ...

'Help!' I screamed to Phredde.

'What's wrong?' cried Phredde.

'There aren't any branches! How are you supposed to climb down this thing?'

'Er, slide ... or ... well, I don't know!' wailed Phredde.

'Then haul me up again!' I hollered.

So we went down the stairs instead.

'Have a nice time, kiddies!' carolled the gnome. 'Remember, dinner is at six o'clock!'

'Don't worry!' I yelled. 'I never miss a meal.'

Then we were outside the guesthouse, in Phaeryland.

three

Dragons and Bunny Rabbits

The birds went *tweet tweet* above us and a few giant butterflies lazily fluttered in the distance. We wandered through the guesthouse gardens (I gave up trying not to step on the flowers). I was just about to cross the funny little bridge when Phredde yelled, 'Hey! Stop!'

I stopped. 'What's wrong?'

'Don't cross that bridge!'

I frowned. 'Why not?'

'Er ... it's much nicer paddling,' said Phredde a bit nervously. 'That's what tinkling brooks are for.' She sat down on the too-green grass and began to take her joggers off.

Well, it seemed a bit odd to me — for a moment there I'd thought that Phredde even looked a little frightened. But that was impossible. It was just a bridge ... and anyway, there's nothing to be frightened of in Phaeryland!

But this was Phredde's country, not mine. So I sat down too (the grass felt like a soft green cushion) and took my joggers off as well, and followed Phredde through the water. (I was getting used to her new 'giant' size by now.)

The cold water did feel good on the toes, and on the stream bottom were little round pebbles, which sort of massaged your feet, too. I could even see a few tiny goldfish peering at us curiously from a patch of waterweed. (If they'd been our piranhas we'd have lost our toes, but I don't suppose they've ever heard of piranhas either in Phaeryland.)

But it was still a nuisance having to put my socks and joggers back on. And anyway, why have bridges at all if you weren't supposed to cross them? But like I said, it wasn't my country, it was Phredde's.

'Er, Phredde,' I said.

'Yes,' said Phredde. By now we were trotting down a long yellow brick road that wound through the trees. The trees had big round tops and bright red fruit on them. They all looked the same. They were a bit boring, to tell the truth. I mean, gum trees have *character*.

'Exactly what is there to do in Phaeryland? Apart from being kidnapped by caterpillars and doing phaery dances and stuff like that?'

'Not much,' said Phredde.

'You mean there is *nothing* interesting in Phaeryland?'

'Not really,' said Phredde, a bit evasively.

'But there must be something!'

'Oh, no,' said Phredde, 'not in Phaeryland.'

'Nothing even sort of dangerous or exciting?'

'Nope,' said Phredde.

'Oh,' I said. We trotted along the road some more. A few birds twittered at us from the lollipop trees, but that was all.

We kept on walking.

'Er, Phredde?'

'Mmm?' said Phredde.

'You know how you said there was nothing interesting in Phaeryland?'

'Mmm,' said Phredde.

'Well, there's something interesting over there.'

'Like what?' said Phredde.

'Like smoke,' I said.

'Smoke's not interesting,' said Phredde.

'It is if it isn't coming out of a chimney and there's no sign of any fire,' I said.

'Oh,' said Phredde. Then she said, 'Maybe we should just back up a little. Sort of get closer to those trees.'

'Why?' I asked.

'Because it's probably a dragon!' shrieked Phredde. 'Run!'

So we ran.

Ten minutes later we were sitting on a branch in one of the lollipop trees peering at the puffs of smoke and I was getting bored.

'Er, Phredde,' I said.

'Yeah?' asked Phredde.

'How come the dragon isn't doing anything? All I can see is smoke.'

'Maybe it's asleep,' said Phredde. 'Or resting.'

'Yeah, I suppose,' I said. 'Er, Phredde?'

'Yeah,' said Phredde.

'You know how you said that everything is safe in Phaeryland?'

'Yeah,' said Phredde.

'Then how come we're sitting in a tree to escape a dragon?'

'Oh,' said Phredde airily. 'Phaeryland is quite safe. Apart from the dragons.'

'And the giant butterflies who think you're an escaped caterpillar,' I said.

'Yeah, and those too.'

'Oh,' I said. 'I see.'

The round green trees looked pretty from the ground, but they were awfully hard to sit upon. Also, it was getting boring just sitting there.

I looked around. The dragon — if it was a dragon — was still puffing away, with little round smoke balloons circling up into the sky (even the smoke is cute in Phaeryland).

'How about just PINGING the dragon away?' I suggested.

'I can't,' pointed out Phredde. 'Remember? Creatures that live in Phaeryland are magic, just like me, so my magic won't work on them.'

'Yeah, I remember,' I said. I was just about to suggest she PING us some nice non-magical hamburgers when I looked a bit more closely at the red fruit dangling on the tree.

'Hey, look,' I said. 'Lollipop fruit.'

'Well, of course,' said Phredde. 'It's a lollipop tree.'

'Wow!' I said. 'Hey, can we eat them?'

'Sure,' said Phredde.

'Hey, cool. Are there hamburger trees in Phaeryland too?'

'Don't be silly,' said Phredde. 'Hamburgers don't grow on trees.'

So we each picked a lollipop and sat on our branch sucking it for about 136 hours (well, ten minutes, anyway) when something slowly began to dawn on me.

'Hey, Phredde?'

'Mmm,' said Phredde around her lollipop.

'You know the dragon?'

'Yeah,' said Phredde.

'The ferocious dragon we're sitting up in this tree avoiding?'

'Yeah,' said Phredde.

'Well, I don't think it's a dragon at all. See, look at the smoke. It's coming right out of the grassy hill.'

Phredde peered down at where I was pointing. 'Maybe the dragon is in a cave under the hill,' she pointed out. 'Dragons like caves.'

'Yeah, but look at that!' I pointed over to the hill. There was a tiny door, about half as tall as I am, half-hidden in the grass. 'If that's a dragon's front door then it's a really small dragon.'

'Maybe it's a baby dragon,' said Phredde half-heartedly.

'Nah. Let's find out,' I said.

I slid down the lollipop tree and marched — well, sort of tiptoed, to be honest — over to the door. It was painted green, the same colour as the grass, which was why I hadn't noticed it before, and over the letter box in the middle was written 'Mrs Bunny Rabbit'.

'Hey, Phredde!' I yelled.

'What?' yelled Phredde, still up the tree.

'Either this is a really sneaky dragon, or someone called Mrs Bunny Rabbit lives here.'

'Maybe the dragon's name is Rabbit?' suggested Phredde cautiously.

'What self-respecting dragon would call itself Rabbit?' I began, when suddenly the door opened.

No, it wasn't a small, sneaky dragon called Rabbit. It was a ... well, a bunny rabbit. But it didn't look much like those really bored ones in the pet shop at home.

This rabbit was almost as tall as me, and had a long flowery dress on, and a little blue velvet hat with its long furry ears poking out, and little blue slippers on its long furry feet, and it carried one of those really old-fashioned shopping baskets over one arm, er, paw.

Cute? Even a preschooler would have crumpled up the page and thrown it out.

'Oh, goodness me!' exclaimed the rabbit, twitching her cute little nose.

'Er ... I beg your pardon,' I said politely (Mum would have been proud of me). 'I didn't mean to disturb you ...'

'Oh, no. Oh, goodness me, no,' twittered the rabbit. 'I am always so pleased to have visitors! Won't you come in?'

'Er, no, really ...'

'But you must!' insisted the rabbit happily. 'Oh, I hardly ever have visitors!'

'Look, really ...' I began.

'Oh, this is so exciting! I'll just put the kettle on and get out some cakes ...'

'Did you say cakes?' I enquired. 'Hey, Phredde!' I yelled. 'We're going to have afternoon tea with Mrs Bunny Rabbit!'

So Phredde slid down the tree too, and we followed Mrs Bunny Rabbit into her hole.

Have you ever been down a rabbit hole? Well, unless you've been to Phaeryland I don't suppose you have. I don't suppose Phaeryland rabbit holes are much like the ones in the world outside, either.

This one was long, and the walls weren't dirt — well, they may have been dirt, but they'd been smoothed and painted pale yellow, and there were lots of tiny lights in the smooth yellow ceiling too, and pale blue carpet on the floor.

So we walked about fifty kilometres (well, maybe ten metres) down this rabbit hole, and then it opened out into this great big room.

It looked pretty much like a normal kitchen, except for the tree roots sticking out here and there (but they'd been painted yellow too), and the fact that there were no windows. But there were kitchen benches, all blue and yellow, and a great big table in the middle, and lots of cupboards around the walls and a stove and a door which I supposed led to a bathroom, if rabbits used a bathroom, or a bedroom, or something like that.

'Do sit down!' twittered Mrs Bunny Rabbit. 'Oh, I didn't introduce myself! I'm Mrs ...'

'Mrs Bunny Rabbit,' I put in. 'I saw it on the door. I'm Prudence and this is Phredde.'

'Oh, I am so pleased to meet you!' said Mrs Bunny Rabbit. 'And what are you, if you don't think I'm terribly rude?'

'Er, what do you mean, what are we?' I asked.

Mrs Rabbit looked puzzled. 'Well, I'm a rabbit,' she pointed out.

'Oh, I see,' I said. 'Well, I'm a girl and Phredde is a phaery.'

Mrs Rabbit wrinkled up her furry forehead. 'A girl? A phaery? But that's impossible!'

'Why is it impossible?' I demanded.

'Well, your clothes ...' said Mrs Rabbit. 'Where are your lacy skirts? Your glass slippers? Your tiaras?'

'Oh, I see what you mean,' I said, relieved. 'No, we're ... we're ...'

'We're in disguise,' put in Phredde quickly.

'Ah!' Mrs Rabbit was obviously relieved. 'What a good idea! There are so many dangerous ...'

'Did you say something about cakes?' put in Phredde quickly.

'Oh, cakes! Of course!' Mrs Rabbit bustled over to the big cupboard opposite the stove. 'Do sit down, girls. Do sit down!'

Phredde pulled up one chair, and I pulled up another. I was just about to ask what Mrs Rabbit meant by 'dangerous' when she put the first cake on the table.

I mean, this was a *cake*! It had four layers, one pink, one yellow and two chocolate, and cream and cherries oozing out between each layer, and pink icing on the top, and while I'm not a fan of pink icing the rest looked *great*!

So while that cake and my stomach were happily combining to produce a bigger and better Prudence, Mrs Rabbit put all sorts of other goodies on the table — pink lamingtons, and tiny asparagus sandwiches with their crusts cut off, and pink lemonade, and pink wafer biscuits, and carrots — well, she *was* a rabbit.

While I ate and drank pink lemonade, Phredde and Mrs Rabbit gossiped about the ladies-in-waiting to the Phaery Queen (one of Phredde's older sisters is a lady, er, phaery-in-waiting). It was really good lemonade, even if it was pink. In fact I'd just drunk my tenth glass when suddenly I realised ...

'Er, excuse me,' I interrupted, 'but would you mind if I used your bathroom?'

'Bathroom?' Mrs Rabbit blinked.

'Er, yes, I ...'

'You want to wash your hands! The icing IS sticky, isn't it? Just over there!' twittered Mrs Rabbit, pointing to the other door.

'Look, Pru ...' whispered Phredde.

'Not now!' I hissed. 'I'm in a hurry!' I dashed across the kitchen and opened the door.

Well, it was a bathroom alright. There was a pretty pink washstand, and pretty pink towels, and a tiny pink bath with flowers on the side.

And nothing else.

I gazed around. Maybe there was another doorway. I peered out the bathroom door and looked around.

Yes! There WAS another doorway. I glanced around quickly. Mrs Rabbit was describing yet another ball dress to Phredde. I dashed for the door before she could look my way, and opened it ...

A little pink bed. A flowery yellow carpet. A bedside table with a book on it, titled *The Little Bunnies Have a Picnic.*

No en suite. No other door at all.

I slunk back into the kitchen.

'Oh, there you are!' trilled Mrs Bunny Rabbit. 'All clean now? *Do* have another glass of lemonade!'

'Well ... er ...' I pretended to look at my watch. 'Fruitcakes!' I yelled (actually I was going to say a ruder word, but somehow rude words turn out polite in Phaeryland). 'Is that the time! It's nearly dinner time!'

'We'd better go,' said Phredde. She sounded pretty happy about it — Phredde isn't interested *at all* in phaeries-in-waiting and ball dresses. She stood up, nearly banging her head on the yellow ceiling, and we trotted out the long yellow passage and out the tiny green door, with Mrs Rabbit twittering at us all the way.

'You take care on the way back, now!' she insisted.

'Sure, we'll take care,' I said carelessly. 'What can happen to us in Phaeryland?'

'Well,' began Mrs Rabbit, twitching her whiskers, 'there's ...'

'We'd better run,' Phredde broke in hurriedly, 'or we'll be late for dinner.'

'Oh, no, you don't want to be late!' said Mrs Rabbit. 'Do come back soon!' she called, as we trudged over the grassy glade back to the road.

'Sure! We'd love to,' I called back. 'Thanks for having us.'

'We'll come back next time poodles do arithmetic,' muttered Phredde. 'I'd rather have my toenails pulled out with rusty pliers.'

'No, you wouldn't,' I said. 'Not with rusty pliers.'

'Well, almost,' said Phredde, as we marched down the road back to the guesthouse. It was late afternoon now and the shadows of the lollipop trees stretched right across the road. Somehow Phaeryland didn't look quite as — cute — all dressed in shadows. 'That was almost as boring as maths homework.'

'Hey, I like maths,' I said.

'Well, I don't,' said Phredde. 'And I don't think having afternoon tea with someone called Mrs Bunny Rabbit is all that fun either.'

'It was a great afternoon tea, though,' I said, burping gently. 'But look, Phredde, I *really* need to find a bathroom! A *fully equipped* bathroom, if you get what I mean!'

'No, you don't,' said Phredde.

'Yes, I do!'

'No, you don't. You just think you do. It's habit. No-one *needs* a bathroom in Phaeryland. Just think of something else.'

'Well ... alright ...' I tried to force my mind away from ten glasses of pink lemonade sloshing away in my insides.

'Phredde ... what did Mrs Rabbit mean about taking care and things being dangerous?'

'Oh, nothing,' said Phredde.

'But she must have ...'

'She was just fussing about,' said Phredde. 'You know what rabbits are like.'

'Yeah,' I said. 'Rabbits live in cages like guinea pigs and eat lettuce leaves. They don't cook four-layer cream cakes and give you pink lemonade.'

'Well, we're in Phaeryland now,' said Phredde vaguely. 'I wonder if Bruce is here yet?'

It sounded like she was changing the subject to me, but when Phredde doesn't want to talk she won't, so I just trotted along beside her as the forest of lollipop trees grew darker and darker.

In fact, it was growing really dark, despite the moon bobbing up behind us. If it hadn't been for the yellow road sort of glowing under our feet we'd never have been able to follow it.

'I wish we'd brought a torch,' I said nervously.

'We should be nearly there,' said Phredde. She sounded a bit worried too. 'Maybe we shouldn't have stayed so long at Mrs Rabbit's.'

'I shouldn't have had that sixth piece of cake,' I agreed. 'It's 'cause there weren't any windows. I couldn't see how late it was getting.' I glanced at my watch again. 'Mum'll be furious if we're late for dinner on our first night,' I added. 'You know how mums stress about things like that.'

'Yeah,' said Phredde. She sounded even more nervous than me, which was really odd, because it was okay for me to feel a bit scared — after all, this was strange country for me. But Phredde knew Phaeryland really well, and after all, as she said, there's nothing to be scared of in Phaeryland. Except for dragons, and kidnapping butterflies ...

'Hey, look!' I cried, relieved. 'There are some lights! That must be the guesthouse!'

Phredde peered into the blackness. 'It doesn't look like the guesthouse to me. It's the wrong shape ...'

'Welcome!' cried a cheery old voice in the darkness.

'Er, hi,' I said. 'Is this the Sweet Pea Guesthouse?'

'No, dearie, this is my delicious gingerbread cottage!' said the cheery old voice. 'Why don't you come in and have a nibble?'

'No, thanks,' I said politely. 'I'm full of cream cake and lamingtons and pink lemonade and carrots.'

'Carrots?' asked the voice. It sounded a bit puzzled.

'It was at a rabbit's. But thank you all the same. Er ... you don't have a bathroom, do you?'

'A bathroom? But of course ...' I could see a sweet, wrinkly smile now, and a hint of white hair in the darkness. 'Would you like to use my bathroom?'

I suddenly realised I'd have to be a bit more specific. 'I mean a ... a ...' I frantically tried to think of the polite word for it, 'a lavatory!'

'Well, no, dear.' The sweet little old voice sounded a bit puzzled now. 'I don't think I have one of those. Is it a type of biscuit?'

'No. It's a ... a ... Never mind,' I said quickly.

'But I do have lots of gingerbread! A whole house of gingerbread! Won't you come and taste it?'

'No thanks,' I said. 'We really have to be getting back.'

'But it's such delicious gingerbread, dearie!' said the voice, a bit frantic now. 'Such yummy, yummy gingerbread ...' The voice faded behind us as we hurried on.

'You know,' said Phredde thoughtfully, 'I don't remember a gingerbread cottage on this road.'

'Me either,' I said. 'We must have been looking the other way. Anyway, I don't like ginger much Hey, look, there's the guesthouse!'

It really was the guesthouse this time, all floodlit (pink) with a cheery elf orchestra perched on giant mushrooms all around the garden sawing away at this really old-fashioned music. (It sounded rather nice, actually, but if you say I said that to Phredde or Bruce I'll spit.)

So we took off our joggers and waded through the stream and put them on again (even though my feet were still wet) and padded up the stairs into the guesthouse.

We were home.

four

Bruce Arrives, and the Three Fat Hogs

Dinner was ... interesting.

First of all, Bruce had arrived. Meals with Bruce are always interesting, ever since Bruce decided he'd rather be a frog than a phaery prince. This means that he eats mosquitoes and flies and little buzzing things, instead of normal food like pizza and spaghetti, which would be okay if he ate his mozzies with a knife and fork like everyone else. But Bruce eats frog fashion — he darts his long tongue out and goes *glop* — which believe me doesn't really give you an appetite for roast gryphon, which was on the menu at the Sweet Pea Guesthouse that night.

So there we were at this long table — Phredde and I back in our ball dresses and tiaras, and Mum and Phredde's mum and Bruce's mum all in lace and diamonds too, and the dads in their tights and feathers trying not to look embarrassed. *And* Bruce was the same size as me now he was in Phaeryland (he was the same size as Phredde back home), all brown and damp and pulsating, but with a velvet hat with a feather in it on top of his froggy head, because even Bruce has to dress for dinner in Phaeryland.

And down the other end of the table were assorted phaeries and gnomes — oh, and a handsome prince (a real one, not one that had been turned into a frog) and ... and ...

'Hey, Dad,' I whispered, 'what are those things?'

'I think they're the three little pigs,' Dad whispered back. 'Like in the story book.'

'But they're not little at all!' I protested. 'They're great fat porkers!'

In fact they were the biggest, fattest hogs I'd ever seen, and they were sitting right at the table with us. I mean, I'm not prejudiced or anything — some of my best friends are phaeries, and I don't even mind werewolves as long as they don't lift their leg on my bedroom door like one of Mark's so-called best friends did last ... but that's another story.

But even if these pigs were wearing tight checked trousers and even tighter velvet shirts they were still pigs. I mean, I'd never eaten at a table with pigs before, not unless they'd been turned into sausages first.

One of the great fat pigs reached over for a whole roast gryphon leg (I reckon a gryphon must be about the size of an emu), and poured a litre or two of gravy over it. The other two were helping themselves to the roast potatoes — again — and the corn on the cob and the roast pumpkin and the beans and the gravy ...

'I suppose the three little pigs grew up,' said Dad vaguely.

'You do anything interesting this afternoon?' Bruce asked.

'Nah,' I said, watching the pigs shovel peas and gravy and coleslaw into their mouths. 'Just met a rabbit.' I didn't mention sitting in the lollipop tree because we thought we'd seen a dragon. 'How about you?'

'Nothing much,' said Bruce.

'I don't suppose there is much to do in Phaeryland,' I sighed. 'It's all so safe, isn't it? Nothing really exciting can happen in Phaeryland?'

Bruce looked at me a bit oddly. 'Er ... no. That's right,' he said.

Gnomes in cute red suits were removing the roast gryphon and vegies now, and replacing them with steamed date pudding and ice cream. I took a small slice and watched the three little pigs take a whole pudding each and cover it with cream and ice cream and custard and chopped bananas and hundreds and thousands.

'You're hardly eating anything!' said Mum from down the table.

'I'm not very hungry,' I admitted. 'We had this great big afternoon tea at Mrs Rabbit's ...'

'You let a strange rabbit give you afternoon tea ...' began Mum. Then she gave a little laugh. 'But I'm forgetting. This is Phaeryland! Nothing bad can ever happen in Phaeryland!'

Phredde's mum and dad exchanged looks with Bruce's mum and dad across the table, just as the three 'little' pigs called for another vat of ice cream and six more date puddings.

Then it was time for bed ...

'Phredde?'

'Yeff,' said Phredde, brushing her teeth next to the tinkling brook in the corner of our bedroom.

'You know how you said no one needs a toilet in Phaeryland?'

'Yeff,' said Phredde over her toothbrush.

'Well, I do.'

'Bub doo cabn't,' said Phredde, her mouth still full of toothpaste.

'Well I do! I *really* do! Maybe phaeries don't, but girls do!'

'Oh,' said Phredde. She rinsed her mouth out (the foam floated away down a hole in the bedroom wall) and thought about it.

'Can't you hold on till tomorrow, and then go out in the forest?'

'No,' I said.

'Are you sure?'

'Yes,' I said, uncrossing my legs then crossing them again.

'Oh,' said Phredde. Then she said, 'How about we ring the manager and see if he can suggest anything?'

'You ring,' I told her. 'I'm ... er ... occupied.'

Phredde pulled the golden rope by the bedroom door and in about two minutes — two really long minutes — I heard a pitter patter in the corridor outside, and someone knocked on the door.

'Come in!' said Phredde.

This red-cheeked, round gnome face peered round the door. 'Can I help you, madam?' he enquired.

'Yeah,' said Phredde. 'My friend here needs a ... a ...' she bent down and whispered discreetly, 'a toilet!'

The tiny face looked puzzled. 'A what?'

'A toilet!' said Phredde more loudly.

'You don't have to shout it all over the place!' I hissed.

'Well, you're the one who ...' began Phredde.

The gnome coughed politely. 'I'm afraid the Sweet Pea Guesthouse doesn't ... er ... have such a facility.'

'Oh, great!' I said.

'But if I may suggest ...' The face disappeared, then reappeared ten seconds later with this giant sort of fruit bowl in his hand. He passed it in to Phredde.

'What's that?' I demanded.

'It's a chamber pot,' said the gnome helpfully. 'When madam has used it perhaps madam will place it under her bed in case she ... er ... needs to use it again in the morning. Then while you are having breakfast the ... ah ... staff will ... er ... attend to it.'

I gazed at the chamber pot dubiously. 'Er ... thanks,' I said.

'It is my pleasure,' said the gnome. 'Anything else madam requires, she has only to ask.'

What madam really wanted was an en suite bathroom, with at least one piece of furniture that flushed. But it looked like the chamber pot was all I was going to get.

'Turn your back, Phredde,' I said, as the door shut behind the manager.

'Why?' demanded Phredde.

'Because madam is going to use the chamber pot,' I said. 'And madam would like a bit of privacy.'

'Alright,' said Phredde agreeably.

Well, anyway, madam did use the chamber pot, then madam shoved it right under madam's bed so madam didn't get her foot stuck in it when she got out of bed next morning, then madam got undressed and into her pyjamas, which someone had placed under her pillow.

Madam was glad that pyjamas were much the same in Phaeryland, except these had little lambs on them instead of my red-back spider ones.

'Night, Phredde,' I said.

'Night, Pru,' said Phredde from the other bed, just as the lights helpfully turned themselves off.

I shut my eyes.

five

A Big Bad Wolf (Well, Dumb, Anyway)

Ten minutes later I opened them again.

I suppose it's hard to sleep the first night in any strange bed, even if that bed is in a really safe, *nice* place like Phaeryland. It was a comfortable bed and all that, but long after Phredde had drifted off I lay punching my pillow and listening to the noises outside.

The elf orchestra was silent now. All I could hear was the distant *plop, plop, plop* of lollipops falling off the trees, which was sort of peaceful as long as you didn't think about visits to the dentist later.

In fact my eyelids had just slipped shut when suddenly this great noise boomed outside the window.

'Little pigs, little pigs, let me come in!'

I sat up in bed. 'What the fruitcakes is going on?!?' (Like I said, you can't say any rude words in Phaeryland.)

'What's happening?' demanded Phredde sleepily from the other bed.

'Dunno,' I said. 'It sounded like ...' Then the noise came again.

'Little pigs, little pigs, let me come in!'

'It's the big bad wolf!' I cried. 'You know, from the fairy story!'

Phredde shook her head. Phaeries never read fairy stories. 'Never heard of him,' she said.

'Well, he blows down the first two pigs' houses, then the third pig in the brick house traps him when he comes down the fireplace and boils him in the cooking pot.'

Phredde stared at me in the darkness. 'But that's horrible!'

'Well, I didn't write the story!' I said.

'How could they do such a thing to a poor little wolf!' demanded Phredde.

'Well ...' To be honest I'd never really thought of it that way before. Actually it was pretty disgusting when you came to think of it, boiling someone alive, fur and all.

'Wolves are an endangered species!' exclaimed Phredde indignantly. We'd done all about endangered species like hairy-nosed wombats last term.

'Well, the wolf *was* trying to eat the little pigs,' I pointed out.

Phredde snorted. 'If he tries to eat those pigs he's going to have a cholesterol problem. Anyway, you eat pork and bacon.'

'Yeah, but not if it wears shirts and trousers! Oh, alright,' I sighed. 'Let's see if we can just get him to go away again.'

I leant out the window, just as the big bad wolf began to bellow again. 'Little pigs, little pigs, let me come in!'

'Look mate,' I yelled, 'if you go on like this the pigs are just going to boil you in the cooking pot, without even taking your fur coat off, and anyway, some people are trying to sleep in here!'

The wolf gazed up at me, all long nose and furry tail in the moonlight. He looked just like the illustration in our endangered species textbook, except he was standing on his hind legs. Oh, and his checked trousers and sports shirt were a bit different too.

'Um, little pigs, little pigs ...' he began.

I sighed. Just my luck to get a really dumb big bad wolf.

'Hellllooo? Look, buster,' I said. 'I am *not* a little pig. See? No chubby cheeks! No little squiggly tail! No porky chops with apple sauce! The real little pigs are probably fast asleep on the other side of the guesthouse, and besides, they're great big hogs and you wouldn't want to eat them anyway. Too much fat. You'd have a heart attack — you know, blocked arteries and all that! Why don't you go and fix yourself a nice salad sandwich? You know, yummy lettuce and tomato. It's much better for you.'

The wolf stared at me. 'Lettuce and tomato?' he growled, sort of confused.

'Yeah. You know — all green and red? Or how about you call up for a takeaway sausage and pineapple pizza?'

The wolf shook his head in confusion. 'Little pigs, little pigs ...' he began again.

There was nothing else for it. I reached under my bed and pulled out the chamber pot. 'A final warning, wolf!' I called. 'Get lost!'

The wolf ignored me.

'You'll be soooorryy!' I sang.

'Little pigs, litt ...'

So I lifted up the chamber pot and ...

Well, you don't really want to know what happened next. Let's just say that three minutes later the wolf was yelping his way back down the yellow brick road, and he wasn't going to feel like eating *anything* for quite a long time (he'd had his mouth open mid 'little pig' just at the critical moment).

And Phredde and I were back in bed and the chamber pot was back where it should be, and I reflected happily that now it would be quite empty when madam wanted to use it in the morning.

Then I did go to sleep.

six

Breakfast in Phaeryland

There weren't many people at breakfast when Phredde and I went down the next morning. Just Bruce, slurping up a bowl of mosquitoes and a glass of fresh green pond water, and the handsome prince I'd seen the night before, in these really tight tights — I mean, you could see every bump on his knees — and a velvet shirt with sagging sleeves and all these ribbons embroidered up them. He was tucking into a big plate of baked beans on toast and waving away the gryphon eggs and bacon.

And the three little pigs were there too, even fatter than ever, each with what looked like a bucket of cornflakes in front of them, and stacks of buttery toast so high they looked like they were going to topple onto the floor, and six pots of jam and what looked like a bathtub full of peanut butter.

I wondered if I should tell them about their narrow escape the night before — I mean, they might have been grateful or something. But then I looked at them *chomp, chomp, chomping* their way through their six tonnes of cornflakes — their manners were, well, piggish — and I thought, no, thank you very much, however pigs show their gratitude I just don't want to know. So Phredde and I sat next to Bruce instead.

'What's for breakfast?' I asked.

'Fried mosquitoes, grilled flies ...'

'What's normal for breakfast?' I interrupted.

'There's nothing wrong with a few nice flies,' said Bruce. He had to raise his voice over the *chomp, chomp, chomp* of the hogs at the other table. 'Oh, alright. Toasted phaery bread ...'

'Honeydew nectar, scrambled gryphon eggs and bacon, baked beans on toast, cheese omelette and cornflakes,' said the manager at my elbow, 'and if madam would like mushrooms on toast ...'

I thought about the red and white spotted mushrooms we'd seen on the way here. And even if I did eat bacon at home it didn't really seem *polite* eating it next to the three fat hogs.

'Er ... just scrambled gryphon eggs,' I said.

'Same for me,' said Phredde.

The manager had just put them on the table — they looked just like normal eggs except they were a darker gold — when Mum staggered in.

'Gllumpphhhhttt,' said Mum. Mum isn't at her best at breakfast. Even her tiara was on crooked.

'Good morning, madam!' said the manager brightly. 'What can we offer madam this bright and glorious morning?'

'Grrmmmmppphhhh blug,' said Mum. 'Just coffee. Lots of coffee.'

'I am sorry, madam. We don't have coffee at the Sweet Pea Guesthouse,' said the manager apologetically.

'No coffee!' Mum's eyes widened in horror. 'Good grief! Where's the nearest coffee bar then?'

'I'm sorry, madam,' said the manager, and he really did look upset about it. 'There is no coffee anywhere in Phaeryland. We do have some delicious honeydew nectar, though ...'

'No coffee!' shrieked Mum again. She was wide awake now.

'I'm sorry, madam,' repeated the manager. 'But the honeydew nectar is really very good.'

'Is it hot?' demanded Mum.

'Well, I suppose we can heat it up, madam.'

Mum groaned. 'Alright. One hot, strong honeydew nectar.' She shook her head as he trotted off. 'No coffee,' she muttered. She stared at me blearily. 'What are you eating?'

'Scrambled gryphon eggs,' I said. 'They're good.'

Mum sort of shuddered. 'Anyway,' I said, 'what are we doing today?'

Mum brightened up a bit. 'Well, Splendifera is going to take us to have an audience with the Phaery Queen. Just imagine, Prudence, I'm going to meet real royalty! And then we're going to practise the formal phaery dances, and then ...'

'Er,' I said, 'do Phredde and Bruce and I have to come too?'

Even Mum realises that formal dances and I just don't go together. 'Not if you don't want to,' she conceded.

'I don't,' I said.

'Well then, why don't you and Ethereal ... and Bruce, of course ...' Bruce gave her a wide froggy grin over his mosquitoes and Mum shuddered again, 'go for a nice little walk? After all, it's Phaeryland! There's nothing that can possibly hurt you in Phaeryland.'

Phredde and Bruce shared a look across the table. It was just like the look they'd shared last night, one of those looks that mean *something*, but just as I was about to ask them what — and how come they were giving each other these looks and leaving me out — the manager placed this great trough of scrambled gryphon eggs in front of the three 'little' pigs, and what with their snuffling and snorting and spraying scrambled gryphon egg all over the place, I forgot all about it.

seven

Phredde and Bruce's Secrets

So we went for our nice little walk — I mean, what other sort of walk is there in Phaeryland? Or rather, I walked, and so did Phredde (being extra large in Phaeryland meant that her wings were mostly for show), and Bruce plopped along beside us, except when he splashed through the tinkling stream. (I was getting to wish it'd play a different tune now — go *boom chugga boom* maybe, instead of *tinkle tinkle*.)

'I still don't see why we can't use the bridge,' I grumbled as I dried my feet on my socks. 'It's a perfectly good bridge.'

I gestured up at it. It was a really cute bridge, actually, with a wooden top and big stone piers underneath. In fact the bridge seemed about ten times too big for such a little stream — the water hardly came over our ankles.

Bruce and Phredde exchanged another one of their looks. 'But splashing through a stream is fun!' said Bruce.

'It might be if you're a frog,' I said.

'I really *like* splashing through streams,' said Phredde. But somehow she didn't sound as convincing as Bruce.

'Well, I don't,' I said. I was really starting to get a bit upset, to tell the truth. I mean, Phredde is my best friend, and I sort of thought that Bruce, well, sort of liked me more than anyone else too. But now we were in Phaeryland it was like I was suddenly an outsider.

We put our joggers on (well, Phredde and I did, anyway) and started to walk down the yellow brick road.

'Phaeryland,' muttered Bruce gloomily.

'What's wrong?' I asked, still a bit grumpily. Phaeryland was pretty boring, true, but it wasn't that bad.

'No juicy flies. No crunchy mosquitoes,' said Bruce.

'But you had flies and mozzies for breakfast!' I objected.

'Imported,' said Bruce. 'It's not the same when your mosquitoes are on a plate, anyway. You don't get that zing that you get when you haul them through the air on your tongue and they're still squirming.'

'Eeerk,' said Phredde. 'Look, if you're going to talk about creepy-crawlies, you can take a walk in the other direction.'

'Flies and mozzies don't creep or crawl!' objected Bruce. 'They ...'

'Be quiet, Bruce!' yelled Phredde and I together. So he was.

The sun was winking at us gently through the lollipop trees and the flowers glowed pink and yellow and blue and red, and the little birds went *tweet, tweet, twee*t like they'd forgotten any other words in the song book. Like I said, it was boring.

'Hey, there's that cottage we saw last night,' said Phredde.

I squinted at it. 'I thought it was a gingerbread cottage last night!'

'It was pretty dark,' said Phredde.

'But the little old lady *said* it was a gingerbread cottage.'

'Maybe she has Alzheimer's,' said Bruce. 'She just *thought* she lived in a gingerbread cottage, but it was really ...'

'A yummy chocolate and walnut slice cottage!' announced a sweet little old voice from behind the hedge. A face popped up to match it, all smiles and wrinkles and white hair pulled back into a bun and these cute little glasses on the end of her nose. She even wore a shawl with long, drooping fringes. 'That's what this house is! A chocolate and walnut slice cottage! Not a nasty old gingerbread cottage at all!'

'Er, yeah, I can see that,' I said.

Actually the chocolate and walnut slices looked like pretty sturdy building material, a bit like bricks really, except chocolaty, and the walnuts made a nice pattern too.

Apart from the chocolate and walnuts, the house was just like those cute cottages in colouring-in books. It had two windows and a door in front, and a chocolate icing roof, and a little crooked chimney, and a few puffs of smoke all white and round against the blue, blue sky. It was really pretty, though I wouldn't have wanted to be inside when it rained, in case the roof melted all this chocolate glug over you. But I suppose it never does rain in Phaeryland.

'Isn't it a pretty cottage?' said the sweet little old lady eagerly. 'Why don't you all come in and have a little nibble? Especially you!' She beamed at me in a particularly friendly way.

'No, thank you!' said Phredde. She sounded a bit rude, actually.

'Nope,' croaked Bruce, even more rudely. 'Come on,' he added to me, 'we've got to be going!'

'Oh,' sighed the sweet little old lady sadly. She looked at me imploringly. 'You'll be kind to a little old lady, won't you?' she pleaded. 'You'll have a little taste of my yummy cottage?'

'Er, I'd love to,' I said, 'but I'm full of scrambled gryphon eggs. Maybe some other time.' Like when fish use mobile phones, I thought. After the afternoon tea with Mrs Bunny Rabbit the day before, there was no way I wanted another polite Phaeryland tea party. But I wasn't going to be rude to her like Phredde and Bruce.

'But it's such yummy chocolate and walnut slice!' protested the sweet little old lady, a bit desperately.

I started to feel guilty. But not guilty enough to go and have morning tea and chocolate walnut slices.

'I'm really sorry, but we're late!' I said politely. 'See you.'

I set off at a jog along the yellow brick road, Phredde and Bruce tagging behind me.

'Whew,' I said, slowing down as we rounded the corner. 'Is everyone in Phaeryland as hospitable as that?'

'Sure,' said Bruce. He hesitated, then glanced at Phredde. 'But you wouldn't have really gone into her cottage, would you? Not even if you were hungry?'

'Well, I might,' I said. 'Poor old thing. I think she was lonely.'

'But you can't go nibbling on the houses of perfect strangers!' protested Phredde.

'Why not?' I demanded. 'It's not like I was going to guts so much I'd eat a whole wall and the house would fall down!'

'But it's not ...' began Phredde, then stopped.

I looked at her closely. 'Not what?' I insisted.

Phredde bit her lip. 'Oh, nothing.'

'You were going to say "It's not safe", weren't you?' I said.

Phredde exchanged another look with Bruce. 'Of course not!' she protested. 'Phaeryland is perfectly safe. Everybody knows that!'

'Just like little kids' colouring books?' I pressed.

'Sure. Just like that,' agreed Bruce.

'Promise?'

'Promise,' said Bruce. 'Just like the colouring-in books.'

'It's just ...' began Phredde. She exchanged another of those secret looks with Bruce. 'You won't go wandering about without us, will you?'

'Why would I want to do that?' I asked. 'Look, is there something you two aren't telling ...'

'Hey, look ever there!' interrupted Bruce quickly.

'Over where?' I asked crossly. I thought he was just changing the subject, to tell the truth.

'That ... that *thing*. Through the lollipop trees!'

I peered through the green and brown branches with their round red fruit on sticks. 'It looks like a bed! And there's someone on it!' I started through the trees.

'Be careful!' cried Phredde.

'This is Phaeryland! What's to be careful about?' I pushed away a low-lying lollipop branch and stepped into a typical Phaeryland grassy glade. The green grass was as smooth as that really horrible carpet in my Great Uncle Ron's living room, and three zillion red, blue, yellow and pink flowers blinked all around us, so you felt like some mad florist was going to come leaping out and yelling at you for treading on the blooms. There was even a bubbling brook*, just like in our bedroom at the Sweet Pea Guesthouse.

*A bubbling brook goes *bubble, bubble, bubble*. A tinkling brook, on the other hand, goes *tinkle, tinkle, tinkle*. Phredde says there are also sparkling brooks in Phaeryland (they go *sparkle, sparkle, sparkle*), but I didn't see any.

There was also a bed. Well, more like a low table, actually. But it had a sheet over it, and a few bird droppings, and a pillow on top of that with a few more leaves and bird droppings, and lying with her head on the pillow was this woman.

She had black hair, lots and lots of it, all spilling off the bed, or table, or whatever it was, and really white skin like she'd been using triple-strength sunblock all her life and had never gone to the beach or even had a game of netball. And soft red cheeks and red lips, but not like the red lipstick Mum uses when she's getting all dolled up. And her dress was white, too, and long and soft and spilling down over the sides of the bed/table. Her eyes were shut.

'Do you think she's having a nap?' whispered Phredde.

'In the middle of the lollipop forest?' snorted Bruce.

'Well, it's a nice day,' argued Phredde. 'Maybe she's trying to get a tan.'

'Hasn't she ever heard of skin cancer?' I asked.

'There isn't any skin cancer ...' began Phredde.

'... in Phaeryland,' I finished for her. 'Alright, she's not going to end up in skin cancer surgery for the rest of her life. But she doesn't look like she's sleeping to me. Not normal sort of sleep, anyway.'

'How can you tell?' demanded Phredde.

'You watch,' I said.

I stepped into the grassy glade — squashing about 10,000 flowers, but who cares, there were still about a zillion left — and walked over to the table/bed. 'Hi!' I said.

No answer. The woman just lay there like she was staring at the sky and counting sunbeams, except her eyes were shut, which I suppose was a good thing, 'cause too much sunbeam-counting sends you blind. That's what Mum says, anyway.

'I said, hi!' I yelled a bit louder.

No answer.

'Hi there!!!!!' I shrieked at the top of my voice.

Still no answer.

'Maybe she's deaf,' suggested Bruce.

'She isn't deaf. She's eaten a poisoned apple and is asleep for a hundred years,' I informed him.

Phredde and Bruce stared at me. 'Have you gone potty?' demanded Bruce.

'No, of course I haven't,' I answered crossly. 'Look!'

I reached over and shook the woman's arm — politely, though. I didn't want her leaping up and yelling 'Assault!' at me.

'Hey, wake up!' I urged.

No response. She didn't even blink.

'Maybe she's ... dead ...' whispered Phredde, her eyes suddenly wide.

'No, she's not dead,' I said impatiently. 'She's just eaten a poisoned apple. I told you.'

'But that's crazy!' protested Phredde.

'No, it's not. Well, okay, it is a bit. But it's a little kids' fairy — sorry, phaery story.' I suddenly remembered neither Phredde nor Bruce would ever have read Snow White.

'Look, there's this nice old king, right? And his wife dies, leaving him with a daughter. She's called Snow White.'

'That's a pretty dumb name for a kid,' objected Bruce.

'Well, I didn't call her that! He did!'

'But snow *is* white,' argued Bruce. 'It's like saying "rose red".'

'There was another princess called Rose Red,' I said.

'Roses can be yellow too,' argued Phredde.

'Nah,' said Bruce. 'Rose Yellow's a really dumb name.'

'Look, will you lot be quiet!' I yelled. 'Who's telling this story, you or me?'

'You,' said Phredde.

'Alright, then! So this king marries another wife, an evil stepmother.'

'Was she a stepmother before she married the king or after?' enquired Bruce.

'She couldn't be a stepmother before she married him,' said Phredde.

'Yes, she could. She could have been married before too, and had stepkids from that marriage,' Bruce pointed out.

'Will you lot shut your mouths! Please!' I screamed. 'Look, she married this king, and so *then* she became Snow White's stepmother. And she was really cool-looking, too.'

'Who? Snow White or the stepmum?' enquired Bruce.

'Both of them! And every day the stepmother used to look in her magic mirror and say, "Mirror, mirror, on the wall, who's the fairest one of all?" And the mirror would say, "You are, Queen. You're the best-looking babe in the land."'

'Huh,' said Bruce. 'I bet she programmed the mirror to say that.'

'Yeah,' said Phredde.

'*Anyway*,' I went on, 'Snow White grew up and got even more totally gorgeous, and one day when the evil stepmum said, 'Mirror, mirror", the mirror answered, "Snow White is the coolest chick around." And the evil stepmother went totally ballistic!'

'I should think so,' said Bruce. 'After she's programmed it to say she was the best, too. So did she get a mirror upgrade?'

'No! She called the woodsman and told him to take Snow White into the forest and kill her.'

'I bet he told her where to get off,' said Phredde gleefully. 'I bet he said, "Look, evil queen, killing princesses isn't in my job description and I'm going to complain to the union *and* the police, *and* I'm going to go on the "World's Silliest Conspiracies Show" and tell all, and you're going to be up for attempted murder and hauled off to prison, and ..."'

'Well, no. He didn't do that. He took Snow White into the woods ...'

'The sneaky crawler!' protested Phredde.

'AND THEN HE LEFT HER THERE!' I shouted. 'And went back to the evil queen and said he'd bumped her off.'

'I know what happens next,' said Phredde happily. 'Snow White goes and learns martial arts and comes back and goes *Hee!!! How!!! Hong!!!* and throws the evil queen into a barrel of water and ...'

'Er, no,' I said. 'She goes and lives with the seven dwarves in the forest and ...'

'Seven dwarves!' interrupted Phredde.

'Yeah, and ...'

'She goes and lives with them?'

'Yeah, and ...'

'All *seven* of them?'

'Yeah. And ...'

'Hellooo? These are male-type dwarves we're talking about here?'

'Yeah. Then ...'

'That's DISGUSTING,' roared Phredde. 'They shouldn't tell kids' stories like that. This Snow White chick goes and lives with seven blokes ...'

'Well, they were only small blokes ...'

'I don't care if they were two centimetres high! It's still disgusting!'

'Look, she didn't live with them ...'

'But you said ...'

'She just did housework and stuff like that!' I roared. 'Nothing ... you know ...'

'So she was their housekeeper?' decided Bruce.

'Yeah.'

'*Boring*,' said Phredde. 'Why couldn't she have become a marine biologist or a veterinary technician or something?'

'Because she'd never been to uni! Look, will you let me finish!'

'No worries,' said Phredde.

'Alright, then! But the crazy mirror kept banging on about Snow White still being gorgeous, so the evil queen got really suspicious. She found out where Snow White was, and disguised herself as an apple seller ...'

'I bet Snow White saw through that one,' chortled Bruce.

'No. She bit one of the apples ...'

'This girl is dumb!' snorted Phredde.

'And fell into this deep sleep like she was dead. So the dwarves put her on this bier ...' I indicated the table/bed.

'They didn't bury her? Errk! She'd go all maggotty and turn into a skeleton and ...'

'But she wasn't really dead! She was asleep! And look!' I waved a hand towards the sleeping Snow White. 'See? No maggots!'

Bruce peered over at her hopefully. 'No, you're right,' he decided. 'Pity about that. A nice fat maggot can be really tasty ...'

'*Bruce*!' yelled Phredde. She looked at Snow White thoughtfully. 'So these seven dwarves have just left the poor girl outside where the birds could do their business all over her! I think those dwarves sound pretty dumb too,' decided Phredde. 'Surely they had a spare bedroom they could stash her in.'

'ANYWAY!' I yelled. 'Here she is.' I indicated the sleeping woman beside us.

Phredde examined her. 'I don't think she's the fairest of all,' she pointed out. 'Julia Roberts is much more ...'

'I told you, the stepmother really needs to upgrade her mirror,' said Bruce. 'One of those Pentium models, with ...'

'But what are we going to do about her?' I roared.

Phredde and Bruce stared at me. 'What do you mean?'

'Well, we can't just leave her here!'

'We could lug her back to the Sweet Pea Guesthouse,' suggested Bruce. 'I'm sure they've got a room for her there.'

I shook my head. 'Can you just imagine what our parents would say if we come home carting a dead princess! We'd be grounded for *years*!'

'You have a point,' said Bruce. He looked at Snow White with interest. 'You know, dead bodies attract flies, too,' he added thoughtfully. 'We ...'

'BRUCE!' I roared.

'Er, I'm sorry,' said Bruce. 'I was letting my stomach take over there.'

'You keep your tummy under control,' I said. 'Anyway, like I said, she's not really dead. She's just asleep. So — let us be quite clear about this — there won't be any maggots or flies around her whatsoever!

She's just going to sleep till this handsome prince rides by and kisses her ...'

'Oh, yuk!' cried Phredde. 'He kisses a dead body! He's a pervert!'

'But she's only asleep,' I protested.

'Yeah, but he doesn't know that. Oh, yuk. Yuk!' Phredde made vomiting noises.

Bruce took a careful hop backwards, just in case Snow White should start sleepwalking and accidentally kiss him. (I keep forgetting he's a handsome prince. Well, a prince, anyway. It's hard to tell if someone's handsome when they're a frog — although he is a pretty nice-looking frog.) 'What happens then?' he asked cautiously.

'Well, Snow White and the handsome prince get married and live happily ever after.'

'That's horrible!' cried Phredde. 'You mean she marries this pervert who goes round kissing dead bodies? We have to save her!'

'How? We'd need a handsome prince to wake her up ...' I stopped. I looked at Phredde. Both of us looked at Bruce.

'Oh, no you don't.' Bruce hopped back even further in alarm.

'But you're a handsome prince,' I said. 'Or you would be if you weren't a frog.'

'I *like* being a frog!' said Bruce. 'Anyway, I'm not going around kissing any stray princesses.'

'But then she'll wake up!'

'Yeah! And want to marry me! No, thanks. Anyway,

how would I explain that at school, having this princess hanging around wanting to marry me?'

Well, I could have pointed out that any princess waking up and seeing Bruce's froggy mouth — not to mention his big, bulging eyes and damp skin — peering over her would run shrieking into the lollipop forest. I mean, *no way* was any princess going to fall for Bruce, even if she had been living with seven short gentlemen and doing their washing and ironing for ever so long.

'I think we should just leave her here,' decided Bruce.

'But ...'

'She looks perfectly happy,' argued Bruce. 'And you said she lived happily ever after, so what's the problem? If we interfere we might cause all sorts of trouble.'

'I suppose,' I said regretfully.

'But marrying a prince!' wailed Phredde.

'It can't be all that bad,' I said feebly.

'Poor girl.' Phredde looked sympathetically down at her. 'I bet she doesn't know any better. Raised in a palace, then stuck in a house in the forest washing and scrubbing with seven male chauvinist dwarves. I bet they never even made their own beds! She's never had any fun ...' She brightened. 'I know!' There was a sudden PING and she was gone.

'What the ...' I began, then ...

PING. And Phredde was back. 'Got them,' she yelled, waving a fistful of paper.

'Got what?' I enquired.

Phredde shoved the papers into Snow White's warm, still hand. 'A uni handbook and enrolment form, a pamphlet on the top ten night clubs, an adventure holiday guidebook and a copy of *Feminism and the Mastery of Nature* by Dr Val Plumwood.'

'Er ...' I said.

'Don't you see?' said Phredde excitedly. 'This pervert prince'll kiss her and she'll wake up and she'll read all that stuff and she'll tell him to get fruitcaked!'

'But what if she still decides to marry him?' demanded Bruce.

'Well, at least she'll have had a choice,' said Phredde heatedly.

'But ...' began Bruce.

'Alright!' I yelled. 'We've solved the problem of Snow White! So let's drop the subject! What do we do now?'

'Have lunch?' suggested Bruce.

'It's not lunch time yet.' I glanced at my watch. 'It's only eleven o'clock.'

'But I'm hungry!' protested Bruce.

'So am I,' I admitted. 'This saving princesses from handsome princes is hard work. How about we go back to the chocolate and walnut slice cottage? We could have a quick nibble, and ...'

'No!' chorused Phredde and Bruce, sharing one of their secret looks again.

I was getting sick of this. 'Look,' I demanded, 'what's wrong with having a bite of some dear old lady's chocolate and walnut slice cottage? You said you felt like a snack, and ...'

'Well, it's ...' began Phredde.

'It's like this ...' began Bruce, then stopped.

I put my hands on my hips. 'Go on,' I said.

'It's ... er ... just not a good idea,' said Phredde.

'Yeah, that's right,' said Bruce. 'It's not a good idea.'

'Why not?'

'It just isn't,' said Phredde. 'Er ... you might get indigestion.'

'Me? I can eat six pineapple and sausage pizzas at a sitting!'

'You'll spoil your lunch,' added Bruce unconvincingly.

'Look,' I said. 'What's all this about? What are you two hiding?'

'Us? Nothing,' said Phredde.

'Yeah, nothing,' said Bruce.

I looked from one to the other. I was starting to feel really upset, if you want to know the truth. I mean, after all Phredde and I have been through together, and Bruce and I too, like being chased by that ancient Egyptian mummy* ... I hadn't thought either of them would keep a secret from me.

It must be because I was just a normal human, I decided, and not a phaery too. Just because I couldn't fly, and PING things up, they thought I wasn't as good as they were — especially here in Phaeryland.

Which made me feel really bad.

*See *Stories to Eat with a Blood Plum.*

And mean.

And upset.

But there was no way I was going to let either Phredde or Bruce see that.

'Well, who cares?' I said airily. 'Let's do something else, then.'

'Like what?' asked Phredde, looking relieved. Bruce looked happier too.

'How about we ... we go scout around for other trees? I mean, if these trees have lollipops on them maybe there's a grove of ... of tomato-sandwich trees, or celery-stuffed-with-cream-cheese trees.'

'But sandwiches don't grow on ...' began Phredde.

Bruce waved her to silence. 'That's a *great* idea,' he said, a bit too enthusiastically, giving Phredde a warning glance. 'Don't you think so, Phredde?' His look said, 'Let's just go along with it in case she starts asking questions again!'

'Oh,' said Phredde. 'Oh, yeah. That's a great idea.'

'Right,' I said. 'Well, how about you go that way, and Bruce, you go that way, and I'll scout around *that* way, and we'll meet here in ...' I checked my watch, 'about ten minutes.'

'Why can't we all go together?' asked Phredde.

'We'll cover more ground separately,' I said. 'Who knows what we might find? Maybe there's even a pineapple-and-sausage-pizza tree!'

Bruce and Phredde exchanged glances again. 'Fine by me,' said Bruce.

'But you don't have a watch,' Phredde pointed out

PING. A watch appeared on Bruce's slimy wrist.

'I do now,' he said. 'Okay, we meet back here at ...' he looked at his new watch, '11.23 precisely.'

Phredde looked at me worriedly. 'You won't go too far away, will you?' she asked me a bit anxiously.

'Nah. Just through those trees a little way,' I said. 'If I see any ferocious little bunny rabbits I'll shriek. Okay?'

'Okay,' said Phredde. She still didn't sound convinced.

'See you in twenty minutes.' I turned my back and made my way through the lollipop trees.

Three minutes later I stopped, and tiptoed back again. I peered round a lollipop tree. Phredde and Bruce were still in the middle of the glade. Bruce was saying something — I bet it was 'Look, just let her go and cool off for a while' — and Phredde was arguing, but finally Bruce leapt off one way and Phredde trotted off another way and I was alone with my thoughts.

They weren't nice thoughts either. Not Phaeryland thoughts at all.

How could they! No matter what the secret was, surely they could trust me! Or didn't they think I was good enough, just because I was a human?

'Blooming phaeries,' I muttered to myself (I was nearly in tears, to tell the truth). No, make that 'fairies'! Fruitcaking fairies! Always thinking they were better than other people just because they could PING up whatever they wanted, and fly, and they lived in castles ...

I sniffed three times and wiped my eyes. 'Well,' I muttered to myself, 'I'll show them! They can keep their silly secrets! I'll find out what it's all about without them!'

It was something to do with the chocolate and walnut slice cottage ... or gingerbread cottage ... or whatever it was. All I had to do was go back there and scout around. And if I went really quickly I'd be back in twenty minutes and then I could say, just sort of casually, 'Hey, you know that chocolate and walnut slice cottage? Well, I went back there and I discovered the dragon in the carport ...' Or the mutant giant butterfly or whatever it was they were afraid of (being Phaeryland it couldn't be too bad, whatever it was).

Then they'd be sorry, I thought. *Then* they'd see that even though I was a normal, everyday sort of kid, I was *more* than capable of ferreting out any silly phaery secrets!

Huh! I thought. Make that *fairy* secrets! I stomped off.

eight

Back to the Cottage

It didn't take long to get back to the yellow brick road, or to the cottage either. The sun was almost overhead now (I bet it was smiling down at me, too, with a silly Phaeryland grin, but I had a feeling that even in Phaeryland staring at the sun might send you blind, so I didn't like to check).

Little heat waves were rising up from the yellow brick road, and the lollipop trees were drooping in the heat. Even the birds had stopped *tweet, tweet, tweeting*. In fact, the only sound was the rumbling of my tummy.

A bit of chocolate and walnut slice was getting to sound really good. Maybe I'd leave a few chocolaty crumbs on my T-shirt just to show Phredde and Bruce ...

'Why, it's the little human girl!' said the sweet little old lady, bobbing up from behind her hedge again and smiling all over her sweet, wrinkled apple face. 'Welcome, dearie! Welcome to my lamington cottage!'

I blinked. Sure enough, the house was all chocolate icing now, with little flecks of coconut speckled all over it. There was even a hint of cream filling at the windowsills.

'Er ... isn't it a chocolate and walnut slice cottage?' I enquired dubiously.

'Oh, no, dearie.' The sweet little old lady's smile grew even wider. 'It's a yummy lamington cottage! See!'

Well, after all, I thought, this was Phaeryland. And lamingtons are okay, though to be honest I'd rather have had a slice of watermelon. But I didn't feel like asking her to change it yet again, because after all it must be a lot of trouble to change your house from gingerbread to chocolate and walnut slice and then to lamingtons, even if you ARE a phaery. And anyway, a watermelon house would drip sticky juice all over you and the seeds would fall in your hair.

So all I said was, 'It ... er ... looks very nice.'

'It's a delicious cottage, dearie!' said the sweet little old lady, with a sweet, sweet smile, rubbing her wrinkled hands together. 'Won't you come inside and try a nibble?'

'Er, can't I have a nibble out here?' I asked. For some reason I was starting to feel just a *little* bit nervous, to tell the truth

Thunder growled suddenly above me. I looked up, but there was no sign of clouds.

The sweet little old lady shook her neat, grey head. 'Oh, no, dearie. You don't want to nibble the *outside* of my cottage! Lamingtons turn all hard and stale in the sunlight.'

'Is that why you have to keep changing your house all the time?' I asked. 'Because it gets stale?'

The thunder muttered ominously again.

The sweet little old lady blinked. 'What? Oh, yes. Yes, that's it! I have to keep changing my house so it doesn't get stale. So come inside and try my lovely *fresh* lamington walls! And I'll make you a lovely cup of honeydew nectar, too!'

Well, to be honest I was getting sick of honeydew nectar — it's never going to replace a bottle of Coca Cola, or even orange juice, in my opinion. But if I was going to find out exactly *what* Phredde and Bruce were trying to keep from me, I'd have a better chance of ferreting it out inside.

So I said, 'Thank you. I'd love to,' really politely, just like Mum is always trying to get me to do, and opened the gate, just as the thunder really roared.

It was a cute garden past the hedge: lots more multicoloured flowers and grass as green as the forest glades, which is basically as green as any green colouring pencil could make it, the sort of green Mark's goldfish tank goes if he forgets to clean it out.

There was a little crazy-paving path too, all cute and crooked, leading up to the front door, which was painted green with a big brass knocker on it. The door was ajar and I could just see the neat little kitchen beyond it, the chocolate and coconut walls, and bright yellow table and chairs — not made out of any food at all that I could tell, unless they were made of solid custard (yuk!) — and a yellow kettle on the stove.

It all looked sweet and innocent, and suddenly I was sure that whatever Phredde and Bruce were keeping from me, it had nothing to do with this dear little old lady and her sweet little cottage, which meant I'd better get back to them before they realised I was gone and, anyway, it sounded like it was going to rain.

I turned round just as the thunder roared again. 'Er, look, I just remembered,' I said. 'I'm meant to meet my friends in a few minutes, and ...'

The sweet little old lady's face fell. 'Oh, dearie dear. Won't you just have a teeny tiny nibble? Just a little itsy bitsy nibble?'

'Well ...' I said. After all, she was a sweet little old lady. She was probably really lonely, and it wouldn't take very long to just take a nibble of her kitchen walls, would it? Just a tiny little nibble ...

'Okay,' I said. I stood back politely to let her past. 'After you.'

'Oh, no, dearie,' she insisted. 'You go first.'

'Alright,' I said. I pushed the door further open and stepped into the sweet yellow kitchen, and ...

BANG! The door slammed behind me. BOOOOOMMMMMMMM! The thunder growled so loudly this time it rattled the jug on the stove.

'Hey, what the ...' I began. I turned round and tried the door.

It didn't open.

'Heh, heh, heh, heh! Got you!' shrieked the little old lady jubilantly from somewhere out in the garden. Suddenly she didn't sound sweet at all. The thunder gave a little snicker too.

'Let me out!' I screamed.

No answer, unless you counted another evil chuckle, plus more thunder.

'Look, I'm just a harmless kid! There's no need to lock me up!'

Another evil chuckle, but this one was even chucklier, as though I had said something really funny. 'I *like* human children!' cried the sweet little old lady.

'Then let me out!' I screamed.

'I like them fried ... or casseroled ... or roasted, especially when they're nice and tender ...'

It was about then I realised that this was no nice little old lady. In fact, I was in real trouble ...

'My friends will come looking for me soon!' I threatened.

'Will they, dearie?' said the little old lady's voice, sounding quite different now. 'I don't think they'll recognise you. Not if you've been turned into spaghetti sauce with human meatballs, or a lovely human and mushroom pie!'

'Oh, yes, they will!' I announced. 'They'll get here before you can do a thing to me!' But my voice didn't sound very confident. Phredde and Bruce *would* come looking for me. But they'd think I was lost in the lollipop forest. It might be hours before they thought of looking for me here, and who knows what recipe the sweet little old, er, the not sweet at all evil phaery would have chosen to cook me in by then.

I tried the door handle again, but it wouldn't turn. I banged on the door instead, then kicked it, but nothing happened. I ran at the door, *bang! crash!* just like they do on TV police shows, but all I got was a bruised elbow.

I turned round. There had to be some other way out! A window perhaps? Nope. No windows. The ones I'd seen outside must have been just for show. There wasn't even a door leading to another room.

But there was no need to panic. Absolutely no need to panic. I just had to keep my head. After all, this was just a lamington house. I could munch my way through the walls. Okay, it'd mean I probably wouldn't be able to fit in any lunch or dinner, and would be so sick of lamingtons I'd never be able to walk past a cake shop again, but at least I'd be free.

That wall, perhaps? After all, how long could it take to munch through a lamington wall? I headed over to the wall by the stove, when suddenly, BBBOOOOOOOOMMMMMMM! The thunder roared again.

PING! The lamington walls were gone. The stove was gone too, and its yellow kettle. The table was gone. The chairs were gone. Even the green painted door had vanished.

In their place was darkness, thick and damp and horrid. Dimly I could see walls on either side of me — black, damp walls — and the floor looked cold and black as well.

'Fruitcakes!' I yelled, which wasn't what I meant to say at all, but like I said, bad language just turns into something else in Phaeryland.

If I was still in Phaeryland.

If I wasn't about to be eaten or tortured.

Or even worse, just left here in the darkness till I melted into a little puddle of darkness, too.

And I bet there wasn't a lavatory here either!

'Fruitcakes!' I muttered again, but it came out more like 'Mmmpphh', 'cause I was crying too hard not to even swear.

nine

In the Dungeon of Doom

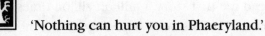

'Nothing can hurt you in Phaeryland.'

'You are perfectly safe in Phaeryland.'

I'd been really dumb.

Phaeryland was just like the picture books, right? Castles and the Phaery Queen and fairies, alright, phaeries!

Something squeaked above me. A bat probably. I ignored it. Something squeaked below me. A mouse, I supposed. I *tried* to ignore that, too, but somehow mice in dungeons aren't as cute as white mice in little cages. The thunder gave a little mutter, but I was getting used to that.

Okay, so no one ever got skin cancer in Phaeryland, and phaeries didn't need anything rude like bathrooms with the most important item. But those little kids' stories also had evil phaery godmothers who bewitched perfectly decent princesses so they fell asleep for a hundred years when they pricked their finger on a spinning wheel. There was the evil phaery who imprisoned Rapunzel. There was the evil stepmother who poisoned Snow White.

'Fool!' I yelled to myself. 'We even saw Snow White!! That should have given you a clue that not everything was safe in Phaeryland!'

There was even a story about the evil phaery who lived in a gingerbread cottage and lured in kids and ... and ...

I gulped. I had been *dumber* than dumb ... (The thunder muttered a bit as though it agreed.) Mum had read me that story a million zillion times. The evil phaery lured kids into her gingerbread house then boiled them up in a cauldron and ate them, till two smarter than average kids had shoved her in her own oven.

Well, those kids had been smarter than *me*, anyway. I'd gone skipping into that lamington cottage like I was on my way to the video bar. I'd come zapping off to Phaeryland without even reading a *guidebook*, for Pete's sake. I should at least have done some basic research first! Checked out a few library books of phaery stories. Looked up some phaery sites on the Internet. Made some notes on the hidden hazards of Phaeryland and how to avoid them. I *deserved* to be ...

I took a deep breath. No, I did *not* deserve to be casseroled up in a cauldron ... or whatever other horrible fate that sweet (huh!) old lady had planned for me. I'd been silly, that was all. But now I had to escape! I was going to escape!

Definitely.

Somehow.

Almost certainly.

Probably, anyway.

The thunder chuckled outside the dungeon. A bat squeaked. Probably a vampire bat, who'd suck my blood so there'd be none left for the sweet little old lady, and that would show her, I thought, but it wouldn't be much use to me.

I mustn't panic. That was it. I mustn't panic. If that movie hero could escape from ninety-six evil ninjas I could escape from this ...

The thunder muttered above me. I looked around. My eyes were adjusting to the gloom now. I stepped forward cautiously, my hands out in front of me.

One step, two steps, four, five, six ... my hands met something slimy. I jerked them back, then gingerly felt forward again. Walls ... concrete or stone, or something else cold and damp. No sign of a window, but then it might be dark outside wherever I was, so maybe I wouldn't see light coming from a window, or a door. I'd have to feel it.

I stepped slowly round to the left, feeling as I went. Blank wall, blank wall, blank wall, blank wall. One corner, two corners, three, four ... I'm not the greatest at geometry (you ask Mrs Olsen*) but even I knew that

*Our vampire school teacher. See all the *Stories to Eat With* books.

a square has four corners, and this room seemed square — although it was pretty hard in the absolute darkness to tell when I was back at my first corner. Maybe it was a hexagon or an octagon or a trapezium ... I was running out of geometry, but I suddenly remembered that if they were right angles (and they felt like right angles) then there could only be four of them. Mrs Olsen would have been proud of me — *will* be proud of me when I get out of here, I thought.

No easy way out through doors or windows, anyway. If it needed magic to get in and out of here I was *really* stuck.

Maybe I could jump on my gaoler's back when they came in to feed me. If they ever did decide to feed me. Maybe they'd leave me starving here, till I was just bones and jeans and T-shirt. Or maybe they'd PING me a crust of mouldy bread, and I'd have to lick the slimy water from the walls to stay alive.

No way — they'd want me *fat* and tender. I'd probably be stuffed with loaves of bread soaked in peanut oil and ... and ... fried chicken and soggy chips and sweet and sour blobs of fat and other food specially designed to make me pudgy ...

Stop it! I yelled at myself. Forget about mouldy bread and slimy water and being boiled in cauldrons and stuffed with calories and having my toenails pulled out with red-hot pliers, and Prudence patties and hamburgers with Prudence sauce. Just concentrate on getting out!

Maybe there was a hole in the ceiling! I gazed up

at it. Nothing. Just blackness. Really *deep* blackness. Either there was no hole or it was so far up there was no way I could reach it, unless I grew wings or turned into a grasshopper.

I hadn't felt any nice trapdoor in the floor in my searches, either. Just the chilly water seeping down the walls, and ...

'Fruitcake!' I yelled. 'Where's the water going?'

The water was seeping down the walls. But there wasn't a puddle building up over my ankles. So it must be seeping down *to* somewhere.

Of course, it could just be soaking into the ground. But the floor was stone or concrete and water doesn't soak into those. Not much, anyway.

Maybe there was a secret tunnel under my dungeon floor. Dungeons *always* had secret tunnels. At least, they did in phaery stories, and this was Phaeryland!

The thunder muttered outside as though it was getting bored. A vampire bat — if it *was* a vampire bat — flapped lazily round the ceiling.

Right, I told myself. All you have to do is find the secret tunnel. Easy!

Except finding the secret tunnel meant kneeling down on that cold, slimy floor. With mice. And probably vampire bat droppings, if those little squeaky things above me were bats (at least, I hoped they were bats — I didn't like to think what else they could be).

Come on, don't be stupid, I told myself. Tracksuit pants can be washed. So can skin. But Prudences can't be unboiled once they've been shoved into a wicked phaery's cauldron and made into Prudence pies.

I knelt down. It was just as bad as I thought it would be. There were at least ten centimetres of yuk on that floor and I *hoped* most of it was slime. I dipped my hands into the ooze and began to feel around.

Stone. This floor was definitely made of stone. Which meant if all the phaery stories Mum had ever read me were correct, there was a great big iron ring in one of the stones somewhere under all this gunk.

There was. Well, it was a ring anyway, and it was big and set in a giant stone, and I supposed it was iron. And if I pulled it, then ...

I stuck my fingers through the ring and pulled. Nothing happened. I pulled again. Still nothing.

I sat back in the ooze and thought. I *must* be able to pull up the ring! After all, skinny dumb princesses with golden hair pulled up rings and escaped through secret tunnels all the time, and I bet they didn't play netball three times a week like me and practise martial arts in front of their videos. If they could manage to pull up a dungeon floor ring, I certainly could.

I pulled again. It didn't move.

Maybe I had to say a magic word. Or be a princess with golden hair. Or maybe it only worked on Tuesdays and this was Friday. Or ...

Or maybe if I (eerk) scooped the gunk away from the edges of the stone it might lift more easily.

I searched in my pockets. This was the time to use my Swiss army knife. Or my nail file. Or the pair of scissors I had accidentally dropped in my pocket this morning.

Except I hadn't dropped in any scissors. I'd left my Swiss army knife at home. And I don't even own a nail file.

Which just left my fingers. And ten centimetres of goo.

Well, it wasn't going to get any less gooey. And the longer I waited, the more likely it was that some not-so-sweet old lady was going to come banging along with her cauldron and turn me into Prudence soup with dumplings.

I started poking. Seven broken fingernails later, and about two zillion buckets of goo, I tried pulling the ring again.

Nothing. Nothing ... and then it moved ... slowly at first, then suddenly WHUNK! it came up and I went down. And the secret passage was open.

If it *was* a secret passage, I thought, and not just a hole down to another dungeon. Or a sort of dungeon plumbing system, so the prisoners didn't drown before their gaoler could turn them into roast Prudence with mint sauce, or vine leaves stuffed with minced Prudence ...

I stuck my head down into the hole. I thought it would be even blacker than my dungeon down there, but there was a faint greenish light from all around. Of course, I thought. In all the best phaery tales there's always strange phosphorescent slime on the secret passage walls that glows in the dark, just in case the princess forgets her torch.

But even with the strange green light (or perfectly normal green light, if you read phaery stories) I still couldn't see much. Like how deep the hole was. Like could I drop down into it without breaking two legs, one arm and a few other bones as well.

But even jumping into darkness was better than becoming Prudence pikelets. So I jumped, well, slithered, anyway, down the edge of the hole and into the cold, green dimness.

The thunder shrieked so loud the air seemed to vibrate around me.

Down down d ... actually it wasn't very far at all.

I landed *thump* in ankle-deep cold water (which didn't matter, 'cause my joggers were pretty much wet with yuk anyway), with no bones broken whatsoever. And wherever this led to, at least it was a tunnel.

At least something had gone right.

I peered into the dimness. More dimness.

I peered the other way. Even more dimness.

Left, or right? Well, 'right' was good, wasn't it? Mum was always drumming 'do the right thing, Prudence' into me. And I was the good guy here, and the evil phaery was definitely the bad guy. So I'd go to the right.

I lifted up my soggy feet, and began to clop through the water as the thunder gave a satisfied BOOOM! outside.

ten

Down the Slimy Tunnel

Something squeaked near my feet. A big squeak. Not a mouse-like squeak. Not a bat-like squeak. This was a ... a ... a rat sort of squeak. A giant rat with long rat teeth and slimy fur and ...

Stop it! I told myself. There are no rats here. And even if there are, aren't rats better than becoming Prudence pate? Prudence patty cakes? Prudence with pears and custard?

Squeak!!

I gulped. 'You be careful, rat!' I announced a bit shakily. 'I ... I'm bigger than you!'

Squeak!

'If my big brother was here, he'd *eat* you!' I yelled. 'My big brother is a werewolf and he *loves* chasing rats!'

Actually Mark has a pet rat called Ginger. Mark would never eat a rat. He prefers corgis and Persian kittens. But I hoped the rat didn't know that.

SQUEAK!!

'And if my friends Phredde and Bruce were here they'd change you into a flea! So there!'

Squeak squeak SQUEAK!

I gulped again. Maybe if I sang, I thought. I wouldn't hear the rat then.

'This old man, he played one, he played ...'

My voice boomed and echoed in the tunnel. Then it suddenly occurred to me that if you are trying to escape quietly out a secret tunnel from a Prudence-eating evil phaery, loud singing might not be such a brilliant idea.

I stopped singing and kept on wading. Slosh, slosh, slosh ...

At least my singing seemed to have frightened the rat away. If it *had* been a rat. If it hadn't been a ... a ... a vampire slug, about to suck my life blood out my ankles. Or a strand of sentient slime that had mutated in the ooze and was going to slime up my legs and strangle me and then digest me till I was slime as well ...

Be quiet, Prudence! I told myself. Stop imagining things! Just because you've been imprisoned in a dark, dismal dungeon by an evil phaery who wants to turn you into Kentucky Fried Prudence, and now you're sloshing down a slimy secret tunnel with rats and ooze and ... and ... and *things*, there's no reason to get all panicky. Just calm down. Calm down and keep wading.

Slosh, slosh, slosh ...

My feet were getting cold. My nose was even colder.

Slosh, slosh, slosh ...

I was hungry, too. If only I'd had time for even a quick nibble of the lamington walls before they'd been PINGED away! Even a crumb of gingerbread windowsill ...

And I was scared! Who knew where this silly secret tunnel led! Maybe I was just heading down into the evil phaery's kitchen. The cauldron would be simmering away, just waiting for her to add a cup of chicken stock, three onions, a clove of garlic and a Prudence!

Should I head back the other way? But that might be even worse! Actually it was hard to think of anything worse. But there was still nothing else I could really do.

So I kept on wading. *Slosh, slosh, slish, slosh, slish, slosh ...*

I stopped. Except the sloshing didn't stop. Even with my feet totally, absolutely still something was still sloshing up the tunnel.

Slosh, slosh, slish, slish, slosh ...

It was getting closer, too ...

I had to run! Even if all that awaited me down the end of this tunnel was an evil phaery cook waiting to make a few bowls of Prudence pasta, I had to get away from whatever was slish, sloshing behind me!

Slosh, slosh, slish, slish, slosh ...

My feet were frozen. My breath seemed frozen too. Move! I yelled to myself. Move, or it'll get you!

And suddenly my feet were moving, *slosh, slosh, slosh*, and my breath was panting too, and I was running, running, running up that dismal secret passage with the slimy water splashing at my knees.

I couldn't hear the splosh behind me now. I couldn't hear anything except my heartbeat, *bang, bang, bang*, my breath tearing at my lungs, my pounding feet. There was no way I could hear anything else now.

'Pruuuudeeeence ...' the voice moaned down the tunnel. 'Pruuuudeeeence ...'

It knew who I was! It wasn't just a giant hungry rat looking for a Prudence-sized snack. It was after me! Which meant it probably had particular Prudence-type tortures in mind. It probably ...

This was no time to think! I had to run! Just run and run and ...

'Pruuuudeeeence ...' shrieked the voice. 'Pruuuudeeeence ... stoooopppppp!'

Ha! I thought. If whatever it is thinks I'm dumb enough to stop just because it tells me to ...

'Pruuuudeeeence ... It's Phreeeddddde!'

'Aaaannnd Bruuuuce!' boomed another voice.

'Phredde?' I stopped. 'Phredde, is that you? Bruce?'

'Sure,' said Phredde's voice, still a bit echoey and ghostly in the confines of the tunnel as she sloshed towards me. 'Who did you think it was?'

A giant vampire rat with yellow fangs ... 'Oh, nothing much,' I said.

'And me too,' said Bruce's voice. 'Hey, isn't this tunnel cool! Did you know there are giant mosquitoes back there? Lots of them! Well, there were, anyway. Really massive, yummy ones. This is soooooo cool!' There was a sort of froggy *splish!* and then there was Bruce, large as life and twice as damp-looking, grinning up at me in the green dimness.

'It's cool if you're a frog,' I said grimly. 'It's a bit slimy for the rest of us. Phredde, Bruce, how did you get here?'

'Huh,' said Phredde — a sort of damp and slimy Phredde. 'Well, we waited and waited for you in the lollipop forest. Then when you didn't turn up ...'

'I knew you were in a temper,' put in Bruce.

'I wasn't in a temper!' I yelled. *Emper, emper, emper* came the echo. 'I was upset! You and Bruce were keeping secrets from me! Just because you're phaeries and I'm not, you think I'm not good enough ...'

My voice died away. After a few seconds the echo died away, too. Phredde and Bruce were staring at me.

'Not good enough!' cried Phredde. 'We just didn't want you to think that ... well ...'

'We were embarrassed,' explained Bruce. 'I mean, it's bad enough being different from everyone else, like only being thirty centimetres tall and having wings and things like that.'

'But you don't have wings!' I said. 'You're a frog.'

'But if I wasn't a frog I'd have wings,' said Bruce, 'and everyone would stare at me.'

'They stare at you now,' I said. 'You're the only frog in the whole school!'

'Yes, but I'm a *normal* frog,' explained Bruce, 'not a stupid-looking phaery with a name like The Phaery Ethelbert.'

'Er ... is that your real name?' I asked.

'No,' said Bruce firmly. 'It's Bruce.'

'But I think phaeries are cool!' I cried. 'I'd love to have wings and be able to PING things, and ...'

'Well, we'd rather be like everyone else,' said Phredde. 'And that's why we didn't want you to know, well, that there are evil things in Phaeryland too. I mean, you're my friend ...'

'Mine too,' croaked Bruce.

'But I thought maybe if you *really* knew what Phaeryland was like you wouldn't want to be our friend any more and ...' She sniffed in the dimness.

'Oh, Phredde, don't be a dope. You'll always be my best friend. I don't care what Phaeryland is really like!'

'You don't?' gulped Phredde.

'No, of course not! I don't care if there are evil phaeries who want to chop me up and casserole me with tomatoes and black olives, then grind my bones to fertilise their lollipop trees!'

'You don't?' said Bruce.

'Of course not!'

'You're weird,' said Bruce.

'What do you mean, weird?' I demanded, affronted.

'You mean you don't care if someone chops you up and ...'

'Well, of course I care!' I yelled. 'Get me out of here!'

'How?' asked Phredde.

'Well, PING us back to the guesthouse or something!'

'We can't,' said Phredde.

I stared at her. 'What do you mean, "can't"?'

'We can't PING you out of here.'

'Why not?'

'Because you've been magicked here. We can't unmagic someone else's magic,' said Phredde reasonably.

'Oh, fantastic. How did *you* get here, then?'

'Well,' said Bruce, 'we guessed you'd come back to the cottage. So we snuck back there, and opened the door and WHAM! We were in this dungeon.'

'It was really creepy,' said Phredde. 'All dripping walls and ...'

'I know, I know, I've been there,' I said sourly. 'Then what?'

'Well, there was this great hole in the floor ...'

'I did that,' I said proudly.

'We guessed,' said Phredde.

'So Bruce jumped down it, cause he's built for jumping down holes ...'

'It was cool,' said Bruce.

'Not to mention cold and slimy,' I said.

'Then I followed, but we couldn't tell which way you'd gone.'

'And then we heard this horrible noise,' added Bruce.

'A giant, flesh-eating rat?' I asked.

'No, you singing. So we knew you were in the tunnel and we followed the noise ...'

'And here we are,' said Phredde.

'Well, great,' I said.

'You might thank us for rescuing you!' said Bruce reproachfully.

'But you haven't rescued me! We're *all* in this now!'

The thunder growled above us.

'What was that?' squeaked Bruce.

'Just thunder,' I said wearily. 'It's been doing that all the time. Haven't you heard it?'

Phredde shook her head.

'It must just be following me, then,' I said tiredly. 'Okay, you can't PING me out of here. How about you PING yourselves back to the guesthouse and get help?'

'Can't do that either,' said Phredde, 'because the dungeon was magic and we can't ...'

'Can't unmagic someone else's magic. Then what *can* we do?' I demanded.

'Keep splashing down the secret tunnel?' suggested Bruce.

So we did.

eleven

The Temple of Gloom

Splosh, splosh, splosh, splosh ...

Splish, leap, splish, leap, splish, leap ...

Splosh, splosh, splosh, splosh ...

The tunnel seemed to go on forever — the green light and the slimy water and nothing in front of us but more green tunnel and more water ...

Splosh, splosh, splosh, splosh ...

Splish, leap, splish, leap, splish, ZOTTTT!

'Bruce, will you stop doing that!' yelled Phredde.

'Doing what?' asked Bruce guiltily.

'Zotting flies with your tongue!'

'It wasn't a fly! It was a juicy giant vampire mosquito!' objected Bruce. 'I wonder what it feeds on down here. Maybe it likes rat blood, or ...'

'Bruce!'

'Well, I was hungry,' muttered Bruce.

Splosh, splosh, splosh, splosh ...

Splish, leap, splish, leap, splish, leap ...

I was beginning to feel peckish again, too.

'Phredde?'

'Yes,' said Phredde.

'Can't you at least PING up something to eat?'

'Sure, I can do that,' said Phredde.

'Well, why don't you?'

Phredde PINGED. Suddenly my right hand was full of hamburger and my left hand had a paper cup of banana smoothie in it.

I felt a bit better after the hamburger and smoothie.

'What will I do with the cup and paper?' I asked, as the final crumb wriggled down into my tum.

'Just drop it!' said Bruce. Even he seemed to be getting sick of sploshing up the tunnel now.

'But that's littering!' I objected.

Bruce turned to stare at me. 'You're in a slimy tunnel under a dungeon heading towards who-knows-what and you're worried about *littering*!?'

'Well, littering is still littering,' I argued. 'I mean, the next person to come down this tunnel isn't going to want to look at my grotty hamburger wrapping ...'

'The next person who comes down this tunnel might be an evil phaery with a meat cleaver and a book called *101 Ways to Eat a Prudence*,' pointed out Bruce. 'Oh, look, I'll deal with the rubbish ...'

There was another PING and it was gone.

Which gave me an idea. 'Hey, Phredde,' I said.

'Yes,' said Phredde.

'How about you and Bruce PING up something else? Something really useful.'

'Like what?' enquired Phredde.

'Like something to get us out of here. Like a map.'

'But if I don't know where we are I can't PING up a map of it,' Phredde pointed out, reasonably enough.

'Oh. Right. How about ... how about a few machine guns?'

'Do you know how to use a machine gun?' asked Bruce interestedly.

'Well, no,' I said. 'For some reason Mrs Olsen hasn't taught us about machine guns yet, remember? But it doesn't look hard in the movies.'

'Wouldn't work anyway,' said Phredde. 'We're up against magic here.'

'I know!' I yelled.

'What?' asked Bruce.

'A sniffer dog! They can find the way out of here ...'

'We either go back or forward,' Bruce pointed out. 'Anyway, we don't need a sniffer dog.'

'Why not?' I said, miffed.

'Because I think we're there. Look!' Bruce pointed with one froggy hand.

I peered into the dimness. Sure enough, the light in front of us was brighter. It looked yellowish, too, not green at all. I could just make out big grey steps leading upwards, out of the tunnel.

'Free!' I yelled.

'Shh,' hissed Bruce. 'They might hear you!'

'Who?'

'I don't know! That's just it!'

'Okay,' I whispered.

We sploshed — well, Phredde and I sploshed and Bruce leapt and splished — as quietly as possible up to the stone stairs. They were even bigger close-up, and disappeared into a big black hole in the ceiling.

I peered upwards. 'Can't hear anything!' I whispered. The thunder rumbled faintly in the distance.

'Me either,' whispered Phredde.

'Alright!' Bruce squared his froggy shoulders. 'You girls stay here and I'll tiptoe up and see if it's safe, then ...'

'What!' yelled Phredde and then remembered the need for quiet. 'What do you mean "you girls"?' she whispered fiercely.

'Yeah!' I said.

'Well, I'm a bloke, so I should protect ...'

'Fruitcakes!' I hissed. 'Anyway, you're not a boy, you're a frog. I think I should go first.'

'But you got us into this!' whispered Bruce.

'Then I *really* should go first!'

Phredde stuck her chin out. 'You're my best friend, and if anything happens to you, it happens to me.'

Bruce sighed. 'Okay, let's all go first. The steps are wide enough.'

So we did. Phredde and I tiptoed, and Bruce leapt. (Frogs are pretty quiet when they leap — you see if you can hear one some time.)

One step ... two steps ... three steps ... four. We had reached the top now.

'It's still dark!' whispered Phredde.

'I think ... yes, there's a door!' I whispered back. 'I'm going to open it. Alight, one, two, three ...'

The door creaked open. *Creeeeaaaaaakkkkkk*. It was the creakiest door I'd ever heard.

I peered out. It was dark, but at least I could see that it was an enormous room, all echoey and gloomy, with a high ceiling draped with dusty cobwebs and windows right up at the top, and indistinct, gloomy-looking furniture too. A few bats flapped through the dimness sort of gloomily as well.

'No one here!' I whispered. 'Come on.'

We tiptoed into the room. The door creaked shut behind us.

Creeeeeeaaaakkkkk ...

'Surprise!'

The thunder crashed! The lights flicked on. They were so bright they dazzled my eyes. When the red spots had finally died away, there was the sweet little old lady.

But now she no longer looked old, or sweet, or even little. Her hair was long and black, and she wore this black, trailing dress sort of dripping all over her, too. Her lipstick was really bright red.

'An evil phaery!' shrieked Phredde. 'Run!'

I grabbed the door handle behind us and tugged.

Nothing happened.

Phredde pulled too, and even Bruce wrapped his long tongue around the handle (and around our hands — which felt disgusting, in case you want to know). The door stayed stuck.

There was a delighted (and evil, naturally) chuckle behind us. 'There's no point in tugging, children. You won't budge it.'

Phredde hurled herself round. 'Who are you calling "children"?' she yelled.

The evil phaery looked a bit surprised. 'Well, you *are* children,' she pointed out.

'Well, sure,' said Phredde. 'But you don't have to sound so patronising!'

'What would you prefer to be called?' enquired the phaery. I couldn't tell if she was serious or not.

Phredde considered. '"Kids" is okay,' she admitted.

The evil phaery smiled again. It wasn't a very nice smile. 'Very well then, kids,' she said. 'You're trapped. Finished! Bamboozled!'

'No, we're not,' I said.

The evil phaery blinked, which must have taken real effort, 'cause she had about half a tonne of mascara on each eyelid.

'Er, why not?' she enquired.

'Cause Phredde and Bruce are phaeries too!' I informed her triumphantly. 'They can't magic you, and you can't magic them.'

'That's right,' said the evil phaery. She didn't look very upset about it.

'So they can just walk out that door ...' I looked around, but there was no door to be seen, 'er, I mean climb out those windows, and go and get help.'

'Mmm? Really?' The evil phaery lowered herself gracefully into a dark wooden chair. 'And where will they get this help from?'

'Er ... Pru,' whispered Phredde.

'Sshhh,' I said. 'The Sweet Pea Guesthouse,' I told the phaery.

'Those little gnomes? I don't think so,' said the evil phaery.

'Look, Pru,' whispered Phredde. 'I think you should know ...'

'Sshhh,' I told her. 'Okay, Phredde's mum and dad,' I informed the evil phaery. 'And they'll go and tell the Phaery Queen, and ...'

The evil phaery laughed. It was the sort of laugh Amelia at school does when she's the only one to have worked our homework problems out right. 'And what do you think the Phaery Queen will do?'

'Er ... send you to gaol for kidnapping?'

'Of course not!' gurgled the evil phaery happily. 'If she could have done that she'd have tried it years ago! You see, I'm part of Phaeryland just as she is. I can't magic her, and she can't magic me.'

'But she's the queen!' I said stupidly.

'A constitutional monarchy,' said the evil phaery. 'After all, what can she do to any of us? She can't magic us, because we're magic too.'

'How about an army?' I suggested. 'With swords to cut people's heads off and ...'

'Oh, no,' said the evil phaery. 'That wouldn't be nice, would it? The good queen couldn't possibly do that!'

'Then what *can* she do?' I cried.

'Just be nice,' said the evil phaery. 'That's her job.'

'Phredde!' I wailed. 'It isn't true, is it?'

Phredde nodded. 'I tried to tell you,' she said. 'Why do you think Mum and Dad don't live in Phaeryland?'

'I thought ... I thought ...' I began. 'I thought they just wanted a change ...'

Phredde shook her head. 'You don't just change countries because you want a change! My older sister The Phaery Milkblossom was kidnapped by a troll, and we had to pay a ransom before it ate her, and Mum and Dad didn't want that happening to me, so they decided to move.'

'And our family castle was taken over by ghouls,' said Bruce. 'That's why we moved ...'

'I ... I had no idea ...' I said slowly. 'Look, I'm sorry ...'

The evil phaery glanced at her watch. 'How touching,' she said. 'But really, we do have to get on with this.'

'Why?' I asked. 'Have you got lots of other people in your dungeons to terrorise?'

'No,' said the evil phaery. 'It's nearly time for *Cooking with Crueliana* on TV. She does such lovely things with human brains ... so I'm afraid we really do have to get on with the torture.'

'But you can't torture Phredde and Bruce!' I protested.

'Oh no,' said the evil phaery. 'Just you. After all, it's *you* I'm going to cook.' She rubbed her hands gleefully. 'It's been *years* since I had a human to torture! No magic protection! Just you and me, and the nose pliers, the thumb screws, the vampire mosquitoes ...'

'What are nose pliers?' I asked.

'Don't worry, dearie, you'll find out,' said the evil phaery. 'Now,' she turned to Phredde and Bruce, 'are you two staying to watch? Or do you want to try to clamber out the windows?'

Phredde looked at Bruce. Bruce nodded slightly. 'No,' said Phredde. 'What we're going to do is ... CHARGE!'

Phredde leapt. Bruce jumped. I waited for the evil phaery to crash to the floor ...

WHUMP! Bruce and Phredde crashed to the floor instead.

'What ... what was that?' demanded Phredde shakily. 'You can't magic us!'

'Of course not, dearies,' said the evil phaery. 'It's a glass wall. You can't get at me, but I ...' There was another PING and I was suddenly next to the phaery '... can magic your friend over here. Now, have you any final questions before we begin?'

'Just one,' I said. 'What's your name?'

twelve

The Attack of the Vampire Mosquitoes

The evil phaery blinked. 'My name?' she said.

'Yeah. If I'm going to be tortured by an evil phaery it'd be good to know *which* evil phaery. I mean, if Phredde and Bruce have to go back and tell my mum and dad I've been chopped into pieces ...' I gulped, and tried to keep my voice steady, '... by an evil phaery, my mum and dad are going to want some details.'

The evil phaery sighed. 'Very well, then,' she conceded. 'My name is The Phaery Daffodil.'

'The Phaery Daffodil?' I asked. 'I thought it'd be something like The Evil Phaery Wormwood or Hemlock or something.'

The Phaery Daffodil looked annoyed. 'Look, my parents didn't know I was going to decide to be an evil phaery when I left school. They wanted me to be a dentist.'

'Oh,' I said.

'Right,' said The Phaery Daffodil. 'On with the torture! Torture gives people such a lovely taste!'

Lightning flickered across the gloomy room. The thunder went *tweet, tweet, tweet* ...

Tweet, tweet, tweet?

'Mordred!' yelled The Phaery Daffodil. 'What the fruitcake are you doing with that thunder?'

'Sorry, Mum!' The voice floated down from somewhere above the ceiling. 'I pressed the wrong control button.'

'Well, unpress it then!!'

'I can't!'

'Fruitcakes!' swore The Phaery Daffodil. 'How can you have a decent torture session without serious thunder?'

'Look, really, I don't mind,' I said politely.

'Well, bring on the vampire mosquitoes, then!' called The Phaery Daffodil.

'Yes Mum.'

The *tweet, tweet, tweeting* stopped. The room slowly filled with a deep, droning, buzzing noise ...

I took a deep breath. 'Er ... goodbye Phredde. Goodbye Bruce. You don't have to watch this, you know!'

'You're my best friend!' cried Phredde desperately.

'If you're going to be tortured by vampire mosquitoes I want to watch.'

'Wow, thanks,' I said.

'You know what I mean!' yelled Phredde. 'And you, The Phaery Daffodil, if you hurt my friend you'd ... you'd better watch out, that's all I can say ...'

The buzzing sound grew louder.

And louder.

And louder ...

I looked around. There was no sign of any mosquitoes, vampire or otherwise.

'Sorry Mum,' came the voice from the ceiling again. 'I think there's something wrong with the vampire mosquito program. All I'm getting is sound.'

'Then turn it off! I knew we should have used real ones!'

'I couldn't find any! There are none left down in the dungeons!' said Mordred's voice above us.

'I ate them all in the tunnel,' admitted Bruce.

The Phaery Daffodil looked more and more upset. 'You plot and scheme for years to get a human to torture, and what happens?'

'I've got some mummies,' offered Mordred's voice.

The Phaery Daffodil sighed. 'I suppose that's better than nothing.'

The buzzing stopped. Suddenly a door appeared in the middle of the room. It opened with a long, deep creak, and the first mummy stepped through.

I stared at it. No bloodstained bandages, no little box containing its brain and stomach ...

This mummy wore an old blue tracksuit, all sagging at the knees. She carried half a dozen plastic bags, too. 'Give me a hand!' she puffed to The Phaery Daffodil. 'These groceries weigh a tonne!'

Another mummy was coming through the door now. This one was talking on her mobile phone. 'You need what!? A sheep costume? By Thursday! How on earth am I going to ...'

'Mordred!' shrieked The Phaery Daffodil.

'What?' called Mordred.

The Phaery Daffodil gritted her teeth. 'These are not mummies!'

'Yes, they are,' protested Mordred. 'It says here on the program, "Assorted mummies, with sound effects".'

'Enough!' screamed The Phaery Daffodil. 'I've had it up to HERE with all this Temple of Gloom stuff!'

'But Mum, it's my homework project!'

'Homework?' I asked.

'Yeah!' Mordred's voice was suddenly really enthusiastic. 'I'm doing a tech course on special effects for horror movies. It's so cool! It's all done with computers nowadays! We have to do this special project for the end of term and I chose a Temple of Gloom, because I thought it might be useful for Mum's work ...' The voice trailed off sadly.

'You're being really mean,' I informed The Phaery Daffodil. 'Your son is just trying to help, and you don't appreciate the effort he's making at all!'

'I'm an evil phaery!' shrieked The Phaery Daffodil. 'I'm *supposed* to be mean!'

'Huh!' I said.

'She's right,' said Mordred's voice. 'You just don't *understand*, Mum! You just keep criticising me, and stressing out when the least little thing goes wrong, like that little mix-up with the giant mosquitoes yesterday ...'

'They were supposed to drink blood, not raspberry cordial!' cried The Phaery Daffodil.

'That's parents for you,' I said.

I know what you're thinking. You're thinking I was being really cool and heroic despite the fact Phredde and Bruce and I were imprisoned in a Temple of Gloom, even if it was just Mordred's homework project. But really all my insides had turned into ice cream with caramel sauce and I was *terrified*! But I thought, if you just keep the bad guys talking, then sooner or later some hero will come bursting in and rescue you ...

Well, that's how it works in the movies, anyway. I just hoped it worked like that in Phaeryland too.

'Well, I'm sick of all this gloom stuff!' The Phaery Daffodil was yelling. 'You just get rid of it!'

'But Mum ...'

'At once!'

PING!

The Temple of Gloom vanished. We were in a kitchen, but it wasn't the lamington kitchen. It was another kitchen entirely.

thirteen

Prudence Casserole

This kitchen was more normal looking. Well, sort of normal. It had nice yellow walls, and cork tiles on the floor, and a big kitchen table with chairs around it, and a stove, and a breakfast nook, and kids' pictures taped on the fridge door.

Except these kids' pictures were diagrams of vampire bats (more of Mordred's homework, I supposed) and the stove was *big*, roasting-Prudences-in-the-oven sort of big. And there was this giant pot on the top, that looked suspiciously like a casserole for Prudences too, and the table was laid for dinner with knives and forks and two place mats, and I had a horrible feeling that dinner was going to be me ...

'Phredde!' I roared. 'Bruce!'

'We're still here!' said Phredde's voice. I looked round. Phredde and Bruce were there behind the glass wall, their backs to the larder.

'Do something!' I shouted.

'What?' cried Phredde. 'I told you, we can't unmagic someone else's spell!'

'Then stop thinking magic!' I yelled. 'Think practical!'

'Practical?' I could almost hear Phredde's brain humming.

'Break the wall down or something! You're my only hope!' I screamed.

BANG! CRASH! Phredde beat her fists against the glass wall, but it must have been super-tough glass (the same stuff as the glass slippers were made out of, I suppose) 'cause it didn't break.

Splot, splosh, splish! Bruce beat on the wall with his froggy fingers too, and with his tongue. It left slimy smears all over the glass, but that was all.

PING. The Phaery Daffodil stood in front of me. She was still wearing her long, black, flowing thing — it would have made a cool dressing gown — but now it had a flowery apron over it, with 'Don't Kiss the Cook' written on it. (I wasn't tempted.)

Even worse, she was holding a giant stir-fried-Prudence sort of frying pan.

'Enough of all this nonsense,' she ordered, 'or it'll be midnight before we get any dinner. You, Prudence, get up on the bench!'

'No,' I said defiantly.

The Phaery Daffodil shrugged. 'Have it your own way,' she said calmly.

PING!

Suddenly I was stretched right along the benchtop. Even worse, my arms and legs seemed to be strapped down by invisible bonds.

'Phredde! Bruce!' I shrieked.

'We'll think of something!' yelled Phredde.

'Any minute now, I promise!' cried Bruce.

'Well, do it soon or *glub, glub, glub, glub* ...' Suddenly my mouth was full of cotton wool.

'Mordred! The cleaver!' cried The Phaery Daffodil.

PING! Suddenly Mordred was in the room too.

He looked okay. I mean, he looked just like a normal teenager, in jeans and a cap on back-to-front and a T-shirt with a tomato sauce stain on it (well, I *hoped* it was a tomato sauce stain) and a floppy pair of wings like Phredde's and a sharp-looking cleaver in his hand – well, an *almost* normal teenager, anyway.

The Phaery Daffodil considered me. 'She looks tender enough,' she said, 'even without a bit of torture to tenderise her first. I *do* hate it when people are stringy. Maybe we could have her fried with chips and tartare sauce.'

I spat out the cotton wool. 'I'm not tender at all!' I yelled. 'I'm really tough! It's all the netball practice we do at school!'

'Then we shall have to roast you,' decided The Phaery Daffodil. 'Or maybe stewed. Which would you prefer?'

'Er ... roast,' I said. It had suddenly occurred to me that if I was shoved whole in the oven I might just be able to tunnel out — or *something* — whereas escaping once I'd been chopped up with a cleaver and covered in batter would be a bit more difficult ...

'Actually, I wasn't asking you,' said The Phaery Daffodil. 'Mordred?'

Mordred considered. 'I feel more like pasta ...'

'Good thinking!' I said.

'With meatballs,' he went on.

I had a feeling those meatballs weren't going to be pork and veal.

'Look, tomato sauce is *really* nice on pasta!' I assured him. 'With lots of basil and nice smelly parmesan cheese on top. That's how Mum makes it. You don't need meatballs at all.'

The Phaery Daffodil looked at me sternly. 'You know,' she said. 'it really does make it difficult to work out a menu when one's dinner keeps interrupting. No, not meatballs. That would mean we'd have to mince her, and you know how messy that can be. I think a nice plain casserole would be best.'

'With tomatoes and carrots?' asked Mordred hopefully.

'And a little thyme, and garlic and celery ...'

PING!

Now I was in the giant casserole on the stove. I peered over the edge ... 'Look, Phredde, Bruce, I don't want to hurry you,' I yelled, 'but ...'

PING! The Phaery Daffodil emptied a really massive tin of tomatoes all round me.

'Yuk!' I said. 'That was an almost clean T-shirt!'

PING! PING! *Plop, plop, plop, plop* ...

Carrots, onions, chopped celery, a few sprigs of thyme ...

The Phaery Daffodil reached over and crushed a clove of garlic over my head.

CLANG. PING! Suddenly the world was dark, and smelt of tomatoes and garlic with just a hint of thyme. The Phaery Daffodil had put the lid on my casserole dish.

'Phredde ...' I yelled

Phredde, Phredde, Phredde, Phredde ... the words echoed off the walls of the casserole dish.

'Phredde! Bruce! Heeelp!'

Elp, elp, elp, elp ... came the echo.

'Globboddyity gloop,' came something that sounded like Phredde's voice from outside.

'I can't hear you!' I shrieked.

'I said we've thought of something!' came Phredde's voice faintly. 'Just hold on!'

'Hold on to what!' A tomato floated past my chin. 'Phredde, it's getting warm in here!'

It was, too. First of all my toes felt warm. Then my sit-upon, and then the tomato juice started to heat up all round me ...

Suddenly I had an idea. 'Hey!' I yelled. 'Phaery Daffodil!'

'I've told you before,' said The Phaery Daffodil's voice. 'A well-behaved dinner doesn't argue ...'

'But I'm getting caught on the bottom! My bottom! I mean, I'm getting singed! I need stirring! You don't want a burnt dinner, do you?'

I heard her sigh. 'Just hand me the wooden spoon, will you, Mordred?' she said.

The lid lifted off me. I surged up ...

Then everything happened at once.

Whoomp! I grabbed the wooden spoon.

PING! Suddenly a pneumatic drill appeared in Phredde's hands.

Gribbagriubba griba gribba! The pneumatic drill pounded into the glass wall separating me from Phredde and Bruce.

'We'll be with you in a minute!' shrieked Phredde. 'Just hold on!'

PING! But before I had time to wonder who had PINGED what, there was a *knock, knock, knock* ... and the kitchen door opened.

'What the ...' The Phaery Daffodil grabbed the wooden spoon back out of my hands and turned to the door. So did Mordred.

'Excuse me. I hope I'm not disturbing anything?'

It was the handsome prince we'd seen eating his baked beans on toast at breakfast.

He looked even more handsome now, with his dark curls and this velvet hat with a feather and his really tight trousers and his really cool black leather boots and this sword at his side.

I've never been so glad to see a handsome prince in my life.

'Help me!' I screamed. 'I've been captured by an evil phaery and she's going to casserole me with tomatoes and carrots and garlic ...'

'And a sprig of thyme,' said The Phaery Daffodil. She smiled really sweetly at the handsome prince. 'Don't pay any attention to her.'

The handsome prince blinked. I suddenly realised he didn't look a very *bright* handsome prince. In fact he looked sort of ... dumb ...

'Um ...' he said. 'I don't suppose she's a princess in need of rescuing? You see, I'm searching for a princess to rescue and ...'

'Of course she's not a princess!' said The Phaery Daffodil, eying him up and down appreciatively. 'I told you. She's just our dinner.'

'Um ... you don't mind if I have a closer look, do you? Just in case? I'd hate to leave a princess in distress.'

'Of course not,' said The Phaery Daffodil graciously, patting her hair to make sure it was in place. 'Be our guest.'

Gribbagriubba griba gribba, went Phredde's pneumatic drill in the background.

The handsome prince picked up his sword and stepped into the kitchen and over to the stove. He peered into my casserole.

'No,' he said to The Phaery Daffodil, who was quickly reapplying her lipstick, 'she's not a princess. Not in those clothes.'

'What! But I've got a ball dress and glass slippers and everything!' I wailed. 'They're back at the Sweet Pea Guesthouse!'

The handsome prince shook his head. 'If you're not wearing them then you can't be a princess,' he said stubbornly. 'My mum told me, "You go and rescue a princess." She didn't say anything about rescuing a girl in green tracksuit pants.'

'Can't you rescue me anyway?' I pleaded, picking a bit of celery out of my hair. 'Just for practice, until you find the real thing?'

The handsome prince looked at his watch. 'I don't think I have time,' he said a bit anxiously. 'I was told there was a sleeping princess around here somewhere, but I must have taken the wrong turning.'

'Are you sure we can't offer you a cup of tea before you go?' asked The Phaery Daffodil, looking even more appreciatively at his really tight trousers and the way his muscles bulged under his silk shirt.

'No, thank you,' said the handsome prince.

'Honeydew nectar? Glass of milk? Mug of warm bat's blood?'

'I'm afraid I never drink bat's blood,' said the handsome prince apologetically. 'Look, I really have to hurry ...'

'Look,' I yelled desperately. (Phredde's pneumatic drill didn't seem to be getting anywhere soon and it was really getting *hot* now.) 'How about you rescue me and I'll tell you where to find the princess ...'

'What would a tomato and garlic casserole know about finding princesses?' snorted The Phaery Daffodil.

PING! BOOOOM!

I blinked. That hadn't been Phredde's pneumatic drill!

Then the smoke cleared and Bruce's froggy face grinned at me through the clouds of disintegrating larder and glass wall. 'Just a little hand grenade I magicked up!' he said. 'I thought it would be faster than a pneumatic drill.'

Phredde dashed over to my casserole and turned the heat off. 'Hold on!' she yelled.

PING! Suddenly I was wearing my ball dress again. AND the glass slippers, which immediately filled up with tomato juice with just a hint of garlic, *and* my tiara ...

The handsome prince blinked. 'She *is* a princess!' he cried.

Well, I wasn't going to tell him the dress and stuff were just magicked up for our visit to Phaeryland. 'Sure am!' I said.

The handsome prince drew his sword. 'Stand back!' he cried to The Phaery Daffodil. 'I am here to rescue the princess in distress.'

'Or in de casserole,' snickered Bruce. Phredde elbowed him in the ribs.

The Phaery Daffodil let out a long breath. 'Oh, put that silly sword away,' she sighed. 'I give up.'

'Me too,' said Mordred. 'I don't like eating people anyway.' He gave Phredde a sort of shy, admiring glance. Phredde ignored him.

I sat back in the tomato juice. 'Just like that?' I said. 'You give up without a fight?'

The Phaery Daffodil sighed again. '*Everyone* knows that a handsome prince *always* beats the evil phaery,' she said, batting her eyelashes at him. 'It's the way it always has been in Phaeryland ... and he is such a *handsome* prince, too,' she cooed at him.

Phredde snorted. 'That doesn't mean it *always* has to be like that! Look, I bet if you went to karate or self-defence classes you could learn to beat any handsome prince! You just need to think positive!'

'Phredde!' I yelled from my casserole (thankfully it was cooling down now). 'She's the villain!'

'Well, she's not going to learn all that at once, is she?' pointed out Phredde reasonably. 'You'll have plenty of time to escape before she learns even a basic ninja leap. Come on.'

'Just help me out of here, will you?' I asked.

Phredde pushed a chair over to the stove and climbed up on it. I took her hand and climbed out of the casserole. *Squelch, squelch* went the glass slippers, as tomato juice went everywhere.

The handsome prince gazed at me a bit dubiously, then went down on one knee.

'Fair princess!' he cried. 'I am Prince Peanut, and ...'

'Prince what?' snickered Bruce. (He'd hopped up on one of the kitchen chairs.)

The handsome prince looked a bit embarrassed. 'My parents had a dog named Peanut. It died before I was born so they named me after it.'

'But Peanut!' snorted Bruce.

'Look, my parents were really fond of that dog ...'

'Peanut, walnut, macadamia nut, who cares?' I said, fishing a bit of celery out of my tiara. 'I'm just really glad you happened by, even if you didn't do anything.'

'He didn't just happen by!' said Bruce indignantly. 'I PINGED him up!'

Prince Peanut looked annoyed. 'So *that's* how I got lost!' he said. Then he seemed to remember why he was on one knee. He turned back to me.

'Fair princess,' he breathed, 'will you marry me?'

'Hey, that's not fair!' yelled Bruce.

'Gloop?' I said. I mean, I'd never even thought he'd ask that.

Prince Peanut looked up at me with his big blue eyes. 'Will you marry me, fair princess,' he repeated, 'and come with me to my castle?'

A piece of carrot fell out of my hair. 'Er, no,' I said. I thought I heard Bruce give a sort of froggy sigh of relief behind me.

Prince Peanut blinked. 'But you *have* to marry me!' he said. 'I've rescued you! The fair princess always marries the handsome prince after he rescues her!'

'You didn't rescue her!' yelled Bruce. 'I rescued her! I was the one who PINGED you over here!'

'I did so too rescue her!' insisted Prince Peanut.

This was starting to look almost as bad as Prudence casserole.

'Phredde!' I yelled. 'Help!'

PING! Suddenly I was back in my tracksuit pants and T-shirt. They were even dry — a bit tomatoey, but not too bad.

'Sorry,' I said to Prince Peanut, 'I'm not really a fair princess. You don't want to marry someone in a tracksuit, do you?'

Prince Peanut hauled himself up, then sat down *plunk* on one of the kitchen chairs. 'I don't *think* so,' he said confusedly. 'The teacher didn't tell us anything about this in Prince Charming School.'

For a moment I wondered if I should tell him where Snow White really was. But then he'd insist on marrying her, and it seemed a bit hard on Snow White to lumber her with this dope.

'Er, how about you go fight a dragon instead?' I suggested.

Prince Peanut shook his head. 'I'm against all forms of killing,' he said. 'Besides, we had a dragon when I was a kid. I *like* dragons.'

'Look,' I said, 'are you really sure you want to get married?'

The baby blue eyes blinked again. His lashes were long and dark too. 'Um, what else is there to do?' he asked.

'How about you jump in the lake,' muttered Bruce. He seemed to really be against Prince Peanut, for some reason.

'Tech college!' said Mordred eagerly. 'I'm doing this really cool special effects course, and ...'

Prince Peanut shook his head. 'I'm not much good at technical stuff,' he admitted.

'Figures,' said Bruce.

'What do you like, then?' demanded Phredde.

'Um ... computer games. Football. Food,' said Prince Peanut.

The Phaery Daffodil's eyes gleamed. She sat down on the chair next to him — really close next to him. 'How fascinating!' she breathed. 'We have so much in common! I'm interested in food too! Stewed brains, finger pâté, pickled toes with ginger ...'

Prince Peanut shook his head. 'I'm vegetarian,' he said.

'Oh, so am I!' said The Phaery Daffodil hurriedly. 'I meant lady finger pâté — bananas, you know — and ... and ... celery brains and ...'

'I didn't know celery had brains,' said Phredde.

I nudged her. 'Neither do you sometimes,' I whispered. 'This is *good*. Anything that stops The Phaery Daffodil from trapping humans with houses made of slices and cakes and biscuits is a really good thing. Not to mention keeping Prince Peanut occupied so he forgets about marrying me ...'

The Phaery Daffodil laid her hand on Prince Peanut's. 'You know something?' she cooed. 'You *have* rescued a phaery princess!'

Prince Peanut blinked. 'I have?'

'Yes! Me! You have rescued me from a life of crime!'

'Oh, yuk!' groaned Phredde.

'Shhh,' I said. 'And that goes for you too, Bruce!'

'I didn't say anything!' protested Bruce.

'No, but you giggled. Let them get on with it!'

Well, anyway, that was the end of that adventure. I got Phredde to PING up a few pizzas (tomato and black olive, and cheese and pineapple with walnuts, onion and banana), just to show The Phaery Daffodil how delicious food without humans in it could be, and Mordred got out his tech college course list, and Prince Peanut got really interested in a course on cake decorating, and The Phaery Daffodil thought that sounded fascinating too.

'You know, I've never really *considered* cooking with other ingredients,' she admitted, 'just humans, humans, humans ... I might really have been missing something.'

'Lentil burgers, carrot soup, stuffed vine leaves,' said Phredde helpfully.

'Flies, mosquitoes, juicy moths ...' added Bruce, slightly less helpfully.

Prince Peanut blinked. 'I don't think those are vegetarian,' he said.

'They're not,' said Phredde. 'They're yuk.'

Which reminded me: 'Hey!' I said. 'It'll be dinner time soon! Everyone will be wondering where we are!'

Prince Peanut stood up politely. 'It was very nice meeting you,' he said graciously. 'I hope you don't mind my not wanting to marry you.'

'Think nothing of it,' I said.

The Phaery Daffodil looked at me a bit wistfully. 'You would have made such a delicious casserole,' she murmured. 'Ah, well, never mind.' She slipped her arm into Prince Peanut's and gave him a long, even hungrier look.

'Er ...' said Mordred. He fiddled with his cap nervously and looked at Phredde and blushed. 'Er ... if you don't happen to be doing anything at the end of term ... er ... all the special effects projects will be on display down at the tech if ... er ... you'd like to see my Temple of Gloom.'

'I'd love to,' said Phredde kindly, 'but I think I might have a lot of homework just then.'

And then we left.

I glanced back as we wandered up the path. It wasn't a gingerbread cottage now, or a chocolate and walnut slice cottage, or a lamington cottage or even a Temple of Gloom. It was just a perfectly ordinary smallish castle with a great fat giant mosquito zooming down at us with its blood-sucking thingummy all ready to ...

'Hey, Mordred!' yelled Phredde. 'One of your giant mosquitoes is outside!'

'Sorry!' came Mordred's voice. 'I must have left the program running!'

Suddenly the mosquito was gone.

'Bother,' said Bruce, hopping along beside us. 'That looked really succulent. I wonder what's for dinner?'

fourteen

Trolls and Salad

So that was the end of that.

We wandered down the yellow brick road — well, Phredde and I wandered, and Bruce hopped. The birds were going *tweet, tweet, tweet* again, and the lollipop trees were rustling in the wind and Phaeryland smelt of late afternoon sunlight and lollies.

'I still don't understand why you didn't warn me,' I complained.

Phredde sighed. 'I'm sorry,' she said. 'It's just — well, it's hard being different from everyone else.'

'No more secrets,' promised Bruce. 'Not between the three of us, anyway.'

'Great!' I said, then reconsidered. 'Well, no more important secrets, anyway.' I'd just remembered the hairy green thing the leftover pizza under my bed had turned into in the six weeks since I forgot to clean it out. I mean, *some* things even your best friends don't have to know.

The sun shone down and the birds sang and finally there was the Sweet Pea Guesthouse in front of us, and the tinkling stream and the bridge. Phredde and Bruce started to head down to the stream. I stopped.

'What's wrong?' asked Phredde.

'You said "No more secrets", didn't you?'

'Yep,' said Bruce.

'Well, what I want to know is, how come you don't want to cross that bridge?'

Phredde and Bruce looked at each other. Then Bruce said, 'Because there's a troll under there, of course.'

'I thought you might have guessed,' said Phredde. 'Trolls hide under bridges, then they kidnap you and hold you for ransom, and if your family doesn't pay it then they eat you.'

'What!' Suddenly I'd had enough. 'No no-good Phaeryland troll is going to eat me!' I yelled. 'I'm sick of being casseroled ... or fried ... or roasted with lemon stuffing.'

'But Pru ...' began Phredde.

'Hey, look ...' started Bruce.

'NO WAY!' I roared. 'I'm going to cross that fruitcake bridge and I dare that stupid troll to stop me!' And with that I stomped across the road and stepped onto the wooden planks above the water.

I was a quarter of the way along when suddenly it

struck me that maybe ... just maybe ... this wasn't a *really* good idea. Mum says I don't look before I leap sometimes ... or think before I go galloping over troll bridges.

I looked down. It was such a sweet little stream, even if it did sound like a mob of preschoolers tinkling their triangles. I could easily have waded through it ...

Still, I was a quarter of the way across the bridge now ... a third of the way ... halfway. Maybe the troll was asleep, or had gone on holidays to Surfers, or just didn't fancy the taste of Prudences ...

'Who are that trit trottings ons my bridge?!' roared a voice below me.

Well, that was enough to make me see red again!

'My name is Prudence and if you don't like it you can lump it!' I yelled. I mean, I was really getting fed up with Phaeryland bad guys.

'Oh, me do likes it!' roared the voice happily. 'Me really *likes* little girls!'

'And I am NOT a "little girl"!' I shouted. 'You can call me "kid" if you like, but anyone who calls me a little girl is going to get my joggers stuffed down their gizzards.' Now I was really getting mad.

'Yummies! Me likes joggers too! They is so chewy!' Suddenly the troll was in front of me.

It was big.

It was green.

It was hairy, with a long tail with a tuft of greenish hair on that, too.

It had horns on its head and great big hairy nostrils — I bet that troll picked its nose with its elbows!

It smelt like the bottom of the school rubbish bins after they haven't been cleaned all weekend. And it grinned at me with long, yellow teeth.

'Look mate,' I said angrily. 'You can just take a flying fruitcake off this bridge! It's no use kidnapping me because my parents don't have enough money to pay a ransom. We only live in a castle because Phredde's mum magicked one up for us. And you don't *really* want to eat me because ... because ... because ...'

All at once I noticed how very long the troll's teeth were, and how round and hairy its tummy was too. 'Because ...' I stuttered.

'Because me'd rather haves a cheese and pickled onion salad,' said the troll dreamily. 'With cucumbers and lots of beetroots and salad dressings and lettuces, them nice crunchy kinds ...'

I blinked, 'You'd *rather* eat salad than me?'

'Sures,' said the troll. It leant on the railing of the bridge. 'Me loves salads. Human beings is so fattenings. So bad for the cholestrolololols.' He rubbed his bare hairy belly sadly. 'Salads is so crisps! They is so crunchy! That's what me does with all the ransoms. Me buys us salads,' it sighed.

Suddenly a small head popped up from under the bridge. It had long, yellow fangs as well, but this troll had little pink bows on its head and the hair on its tummy and even the hair under its armpits was plaited with tiny pink ribbons too. 'Daddy?' it bleated. 'Daddy, have you caughts us someones?'

'Me haves,' boomed the troll. 'How would you likes a nice yummy humans for din dins!'

'But me don't wants to eats a human!' wailed the tiny troll. 'Me is sick of humans! Me wants a salad! Me wants a salad NOW!!!!'

'Oh, for fruitcake's sake,' said Phredde.

PING!

A giant bowl of salad — with pickled onions and chunks of cheese and lots of beetroot and really crunchy lettuce — appeared on the bridge in front of us. 'There's your salad!'

'Salad!' screeched the tiny troll.

'Salad!' boomed the bigger one. 'Oh, you nice nice girlses! We hasn'ts hads a salad for weekses and weekses!'

'Look,' said Phredde, 'I'll make a deal with you. You stop leaping out on people and we'll make sure you get lots of salad. Okay?'

'But how's you goings to ...' began the troll.

'You watch,' said Phredde.

PING! There were two large wooden notice boards, one on each end of the bridge.

PING! There were three pots of black paint and three paintbrushes next to each noticeboard.

PING! There was a hammer, nails and a long wooden stake next to them too.

Well, it didn't take us long. In three minutes Phredde and Bruce had painted 'Troll — sorry, Toll

Bridge. Fee for crossing: one large salad (with pickles, cheese and beetroot)', and I'd hammered the stake into the ground (Bruce's tongue isn't much good with a hammer, but he's not bad with a paintbrush) and nailed the notice board onto the stake.

'Oh!' said the tiny troll still slurping up the lettuce. 'It are just beautifuls! Aren't it beautifuls, Daddy?'

The father troll nodded with his mouth full of beetroot.

And after that we really did go home.

fifteen

Back at the Sweet Pea Guesthouse

Not really home, of course, but over the bridge and through the garden (where the elves were sawing madly on their violins) and into the Sweet Pea Guesthouse.

'Better get changed for dinner!' panted Phredde. 'They'll all have a fit if they see us like this!'

I glanced down at my T-shirt covered with tomato, garlic and bits of carrot. My tracksuit pants weren't much better. 'Yeah,' I agreed. 'Bruce, you go into the dining room and apologise for us and say we won't be long.'

'Hey, how come I have to be the one who apologises?' complained Bruce.

'Because you're a frog and don't have to get changed!' I said.

'Well, if you'd *all* like to be frogs ...' began Bruce hopefully, but Phredde and I didn't wait. We dashed up the stairs and into our bedroom.

A quick dip in the waterfall and an even quicker PING! and there we were all neat again in our ball dresses and tiaras and glass slippers. (I found a bit of celery in mine later but I managed to get it out under the table without Mum noticing.)

Everyone was eating when we finally made it downstairs — the three fat hogs and Mum and Dad and Phredde's mum and dad and Bruce's mum and dad too. (They're really nice, by the way, and hardly nag him at all about being a frog.)

There was no sign of Prince Peanut. I supposed he was still getting stuck into pizza at The Phaery Daffodil's.

'Sorry we're late!' yelled Phredde, sliding into her seat.

'Yeah!' I added. 'I hope you weren't worried about us!'

Mum just smiled over her mushroom and moonbeam soufflé. 'No, of course we weren't worried! After all, what could happen to you in Phaeryland?'

I looked at Phredde and Bruce and they looked at me, and Phredde's mum and dad and Bruce's mum and dad looked at each other too. But no one said anything. After all, we were back safely. And why stress Mum out when we didn't have to?

So we had dinner instead.

It was a great dinner. There was mushroom and moonbeam soufflé, which was big and fluffy and creamy and mushroomy, and stuffed pumpkins, and dewdrop ice cream, and nothing that even *looked* like human brains or roast armpits.

There was a giant lamington cake with cream for dessert too, but somehow neither Phredde nor I really felt like it. (Bruce offered us some of his chocolate-covered moths, but luckily by then we were full.)

Mum and Dad and the rest of them sat up listening to the elf musicians, but for some reason Phredde and Bruce and I were a bit tired, so we went straight up to bed ...

'Phredde?'

'Mmmm,' said Phredde sleepily from the other bed.

'You know those secrets you and Bruce aren't going to keep from me any more?'

'Mmm,' said Phredde.

'Well, how do I know what they are? I mean, if they're secrets then I don't know what to ask you to find out what they are now they're not secrets any more.'

Phredde thought about that for awhile. 'I don't think that makes sense,' she said.

'Yeah, I know. I'm tired. It's just, well ...'

'How about we promise to answer any of your questions from now on?' said Phredde. 'I mean *really* answer them.'

'*Any* questions? I said hopefully. 'Like, what's the answer to question number 63 in our maths homework?'

But there was no answer. Phredde was asleep.

I have no idea if the wolf came back that night or not. He could have huffed and puffed all night for all I cared. Next thing I knew it was morning, and the gnome was delivering our early morning rose petal tea (yuk) and sweetmeats (actually, they're not bad) and it was time to get ready for the Phaery Queen's wedding.

sixteen

Bruce is Embarrassed

Well, you should have seen the Sweet Pea Guesthouse that morning!

Mum was running from room to room yelling things like: 'Nail scissors! Nail scissors! I can't wear glass slippers to the wedding with my toenails looking like this!' And Dad was standing at the mirror in their room trying to stretch his purple velvet jerkin as far down as possible over his yellow tights (like I said, those things are *rude*). And Bruce was nowhere to be found.

Phredde and I got dressed early, and I have to tell you, we looked *cool*! I mean, I usually don't go in for ball dresses and stuff like that (I mean, *lace*! *Yuk*!) but this time our dresses were something else.

Both our dresses were the same, this really incredible gold cloth, all heavy, with sort of embroidery all over it, but made out of real gold, not gold-coloured cotton or polyester or anything.

And our glass slippers were gold-coloured too, which was a really good thing, 'cause feet are very useful and all that but you don't actually want to *see* them all the time, not when you've got a blister on your toe after trying to escape from an evil phaery and it fills up with pus and then bursts all red and ... But you don't want to hear about my blister.

And our tiaras were gold as well, and we had really heavy gold bracelets and masses and masses of gold net petticoats so you felt like your skirt was sort of flying around you.

'Mirror, mirror, on the wall,' I said, 'who is the fairest one of all?'

The mirror grinned at me. 'No worries, kid,' it said. 'You look GREAT!'

I thought I did too.

Well, after we'd looked at our reflections half a million times and practised curtsying without falling on our faces, we went to look for Bruce.

Phredde knocked on his door. There was no answer, so she stuck her head in.

'Hey, Bruce?' she called.

Still no answer.

His parents' room was next door to his. I knocked this time.

The door opened and Bruce's mum stuck her head out. 'It's so difficult,' she said worriedly. 'I can't decide between my ruby tiara or my moonstones and gold tiara or my ...'

'Er, have you seen Bruce anywhere?' I asked.

'He's hopping about somewhere,' Bruce's mum said vaguely. 'He was getting dressed a minute ago.'

I looked at Phredde. Phredde looked at me. Then we marched back to Bruce's room. Phredde flung open the door.

'Hey, Bruce!' she yelled. 'Where are you?'

'I'm not here,' said a voice from the cupboard.

'Well, if you're not here who's talking?' I asked reasonably.

'Alright, I *am* here,' said Bruce's voice. 'But I'm not coming out.'

'Why not?' asked Phredde.

The cupboard snorted. 'Give you three guesses.'

'Um ... you were looking for a spare pillow in the cupboard and accidentally got locked in?' I guessed.

'No,' said the cupboard.

'You're raising money for the new school library by seeing how many hours you can stay in a cupboard?' suggested Phredde.

'No,' said the cupboard.

Phredde and I looked at each other again.

'It wouldn't be because you're all dressed up like Prince Peanut and you don't want anyone to see you?' I hazarded.

'Right,' said Bruce's voice miserably.

'But you can't stay in there all day!' protested Phredde.

'Yes, I can,' said Bruce.

'But your mum and dad ...'

'I'll tell them if they try to get me out I'll turn

myself into a slug!' said Bruce.

'Bruce, you can't come to school as a slug,' I said reasonably. 'Mrs Olsen wouldn't let you.'

'Then I won't come to school,' said Bruce. 'Anyway, slugs don't have to go to school.'

This was getting difficult. I took a deep breath. 'Look Bruce,' I said. 'You're my friend! I really like you! I don't care if you're a phaery prince or a frog. But I am *not* going to be seen with you if you turn into a slug!'

'That goes for me, too!' declared Phredde.

'But I can't come out!' wailed Bruce. 'I look ridiculous!'

'Look,' I said persuasively. '*Every* bloke is going to look ridiculous today! Not just you!'

'Well ...' said Bruce's voice from inside the cupboard. 'If you promise not to laugh ...'

'No, of course we won't laugh!' said Phredde.

'Well, alright then ...'

The cupboard door opened.

'Phhsszzzzwit!' I choked.

'Mmrrgggbbbd!' went Phredde.

Bruce glared at us. 'You promised you wouldn't laugh!'

'I'm not laughing!' I protested. 'It's just a crumb went down the wrong way!'

'I was trying not to sneeze,' added Phredde. 'It's ... it's all the pollen in the air ...'

'Then I don't look too dumb?' said Bruce hopefully.

I looked at him. He wore a cream silk shirt, tight

red silk pants, long brown boots, sort of tailored to fit in his froggy feet, and a hat with a feather in it.

'You want the truth?'

'Yes,' said Bruce.

'The whole truth?'

'Yes,' said Bruce.

'You look like a total prat,' I told him honestly. 'But, hey, *everyone* is going to look like a prat today. No one will notice you.'

Bruce looked at me and Phredde, then back at me. 'You don't look dumb at all,' he said. 'You look sort of nice, actually.'

I blinked. It was the first compliment I'd ever heard from Bruce. 'Well, thanks,' I said. 'Hey, I've got an idea.'

'What?' said Bruce suspiciously. 'If it's something to do with crossing troll bridges or eating gingerbread cottages again ...'

'Nah,' I said, 'this is quite safe. I was just thinking, if you stick close to me and Phredde our skirts'll hide you.'

Bruce brightened up. 'Yeah,' he said. 'Thanks.'

So we went downstairs.

seventeen

A Pretty Cool Wedding

Well, after half a million last-minute panics I won't bore you with (Mum never did find any toenail clippers), the giant butterflies landed and we climbed aboard. We flew really gently off to the wedding so as not to mess up our hair.

It was a pretty cool wedding.

The Phaery Queen's castle looked just as it had last time, like it was made out of icing sugar and sunbeams, all delicate towers and great sloping lawns. The wedding was to be outside, so there were striped marquees (a marquee is a bit like a tent, but grander and with stripes) and elf orchestras on a zillion zillion tiny mushrooms, and the lawn wasn't grass, it was a trillion tiny flowers, and there were bells ringing from the castle towers.

I told you it was cool.

And *everyone* was there. Me and Phredde and Bruce and our families, of course, and Phredde's older sisters, who were okay in an older sister sort of way (I'm *really* glad I just have a brother, though) and 6,782 phaeries all in ball gowns and glass slippers or really embarrassing tight trousers.

The three little pigs (well, great fat hogs) were there too, in *enormous* blue dinner jackets and yellow bow ties with their little piggy tails poking out behind (which actually looked pretty disgusting, but then they were pigs).

The Phaery Daffodil was there with Prince Peanut — he wore his embarrassing trousers like he wasn't embarrassed one bit, plus an even fancier red velvet shirt with gold embroidery; she'd changed into a really pretty pink dress and was leading him by the hand.

And Mordred was there, in normal phaery gear this time, and sort of attached himself to Phredde (I think he had a crush on her) and ... and ... and *everyone*!

Then the music changed to 'Here Comes the Bride' and a million birds all went *tweet, tweet, tweet* and rainbows shivered all over the sky and we all stood back and the Phaery Queen walked down the aisle (this long, red carpet) on her father's arm (he looked a bit doddery, but he made it okay) ...

'Hey, Phredde,' I whispered.

'Shh,' said Phredde.

'How come the Phaery Queen's dad isn't king?'

'Shh,' said Phredde. 'There's always a Phaery Queen in Phaeryland. We don't have Phaery kings!'

And then the Phaery Queen's doddery dad handed her over to the guy she was marrying.

Well, you could have knocked me down with the feather in Bruce's hat!

'I thought he'd be a phaery prince!' I whispered to Phredde.

'No, he's a plumber called Dwayne,' Phredde whispered back. 'She met him when he came to put a spa in the palace.'

Then they got married.

Dwayne the plumber looked okay, actually. I mean, he wasn't handsome like Prince Peanut (and he wore his velvet shirt right down low so it covered up the most embarrassing bits of his tights), but he looked really kind, and like he enjoyed sensible stuff like football and barbecues on Saturday afternoons. He also looked like he wouldn't tolerate any evil phaeries whisking his daughters away to spin straw into gold or cursing them at their christenings or stuff like that, so all in all I reckon the Phaery Queen had made a pretty good choice.

Then we got down to eating.

Wow, you should have seen the food! There was roast *everything* (except for human brains, of course) and creams and jellies and great platters of fruit and vegetables carved into flower shapes and crystal glasses of honeydew nectar and moonberry juice to drink, till Dwayne the plumber had a word with the servants and they brought out some beer and orange juice too, and even coffee. (You should have heard Mum sigh.)

Actually I'd rather have had sausage and pineapple pizza, but it was okay.

Phredde and I sat together, with Bruce between us so you couldn't notice his pants and shirt (he'd accidentally on purpose lost his hat by then). Mum and Dad and everyone were at one of the other tables with some ladies-in-waiting, including Phredde's older sisters, so we were stuck at a table with lots of strangers.

I looked at the chair on the other side of me. It was empty. Then suddenly this dark, shadowy arm shot out and grabbed a sunshine roll, and I realised that there was someone *under* the chair, instead of on top of it.

I cleared my throat. 'Er, hi,' I said.

'Hi,' said a small voice from under the table.

'My name's Prudence.' I was trying to sound really normal, like everyone in our family *always* sat under their chairs instead of on top of them.

'My name's Jessica,' said the voice. 'These are really good rolls, aren't they?'

'What? Oh, yeah, sure. Um, I hope you don't mind my mentioning this ...'

'Not at all,' said the voice of Jessica.

'But wouldn't you be more comfortable on top of your chair?'

'No,' said Jessica.

'Oh. Well, I was just asking ...'

'You see I'm a bogeyperson,' said the voice.

'A bogeyman?'

'No,' said the voice patiently. 'A bogeyperson. I'm a girl, not a man.'

'Oh, I see,' I said. 'You hide under beds and in dark cupboards?'

'And under tables. Or chairs,' said the voice. 'Hey, would you like me to jump out at you and say "Boo!"?'

'No, thank you,' I said.

'Oh,' said the voice, disappointed.

'Maybe later,' I said kindly.

The voice brightened up. 'Really? Oh goodie!' The dark arm flashed up again and a plate of sliced gryphon with baked potatoes and steamed rose petals disappeared under the chair. There was the sound of intense gnawing and a few gulps. Bogeypeople did not have good table manners, I decided. Or under-table manners either.

I looked over at the person sitting next to Jessica's empty chair. He was a pretty short guy, actually, with the pale skin of someone who doesn't go outside much. In fact the other six occupants of our table were short, too. All seven of them were wearing dinner jackets with frilly shirts and pens in their shirt pockets. They weren't exactly joining in the gaiety. In fact they looked really depressed.

'Hi!' I said as cheerily as I could to the bloke next to the empty chair. 'I'm Pru. And this is Phredde and this is Bruce.'

'Hi,' croaked Bruce.

The short guy nodded to me. 'I'm Grumpy,' he said miserably.

'Oh, I'm sorry,' I said. 'What are you grumpy about?'

He looked at me sadly. 'No, I'm quite even-tempered, thank you. My name is Grumpy. It's a traditional *name* in our family. My dad was called Grumpy and my grandfather was called Grumpy and *his* father ...'

Well, the things some parents call their kids ... 'Yeah, I know how you feel,' I said sympathetically. 'My name is Prudence. It means "careful", can you believe it? And Phredde's name is really ...'

I felt Phredde's glass slipper kick me firmly under the table. Phredde does NOT like her real name made public.

Grumpy didn't seem to have noticed my slip. 'And this is Happy,' he said, gesturing to another shortish guy who was busy sniffing mournfully into a spotted handkerchief (coloured spots, I mean, not the snotty kind), 'and this is Dopey.' A really intellectual-looking little guy with glasses and *six* pens in his pocket nodded to me miserably.

I tried to think of some cheery sort of conversation. 'Er, great party, isn't it?' I asked.

Grumpy shook his head. 'I'm afraid none of us is really in a mood to enjoy it,' he revealed. 'I mean, we owe it to Her Majesty to attend, but really ...' his voice trailed off.

'What's the matter?' I asked sympathetically.

'A dear friend of ours ... sudden illness ...' muttered Grumpy sadly.

Suddenly this bell rang in the back of my brain.

'Er ... you're not miners, are you?' I asked. 'And live in a house in the woods and go off to work singing every morning and have a girl called Snow White to do your housework?'

Grumpy shook his head. 'No, we're computer software engineers.' He shook his head unhappily. 'But my great great grandpa was a miner. No, Snow White was our chief software engineer. You should have seen her with a difficult program — simply brilliant.'

'Her loss was a terrible tragedy,' said one of the other short computer software engineers across the table.

'It must have been,' I said sympathetically.

He nodded. 'Our stock fell twenty points overnight on the Phaeryland stock exchange.'

I glanced at Phredde and Bruce. 'Doesn't look like she was stuck doing the housework,' I whispered.

Grumpy overheard. 'Snow White? Housework?' he smiled sadly. 'Oh, no, she didn't do housework. I mean, we all make our own beds. She did do a lovely spinach quiche and baked apples. But we have the Three Bears Cleaning Company come in every second day to do everything else. They're very efficient. I've got their card somewhere,' he fumbled in his pocket.

'No, thank you very much,' I said hurriedly. 'Our castle is sort of self-cleaning. Er ... what happened to Snow White? She didn't bite a poisoned apple and go into a coma, did she?'

For a moment I thought I might be interfering, and he'd just tell me to mind my own business. But Grumpy just stared at me.

'How did you know about that?' he asked. 'It was her new Apple Macintosh computer. This new sales representative brought it round ...' he frowned. 'But I'm sure Snow White didn't bite it. Why would anyone bite an Apple Macintosh computer?'

'A new sales rep? Are you sure she wasn't an evil queen in disguise, was she? Snow White's stepmother?'

Grumpy blinked. 'How did you know about Snow White's stepmother?'

'Oh, I have my methods,' I said.

Grumpy shook his head sadly. 'Snow White's stepmother has always been jealous of her, ever since the stepmother assumed control of the family computer business. She wanted Snow White to stay in the family computer business, but Snow White struck out on her own — in partnership with us, of course. You don't think ...?' His eyes grew wide with horror. 'You don't think Snow White's new Apple Macintosh computer was poisoned?'

'I don't know,' I said honestly. I nudged Phredde and Bruce. 'Er ... will you excuse us for a moment? We just want to see if there are any more of those delicious stuffed nightingale tongues left.'

I pulled Phredde out of the marquee and behind a bush, with Bruce hopping rapidly between us in case someone saw his red silk trousers.

'What do you think?' I hissed.

'I don't even like nightingale tongues!' said Phredde.

'No, not about the nightingale tongues! About Snow White!'

Phredde considered. 'Well, I don't think she was a domestic drudge any more.'

Bruce frowned. 'But it does look like someone tried to get rid of her.'

'Of *course* someone tried to get rid of her!' I said. 'The evil queen! We have to save her! I mean, when it looked like she was just going to have to either keep on making beds or marry Prince Peanut it was okay to let her sleep. But not now!'

Phredde's eyes opened wide. 'But how are we going to save her?' she demanded.

Phaeries! If their parents just read them phaery stories occasionally they'd understand a lot more about the world!

'Look,' I said. 'In the story Snow White bites this poisoned apple and falls into a coma. Then the handsome prince ...'

'Yuk,' said Phredde.

'Shh,' I said. 'The handsome prince kisses her and the bit of apple falls out of her mouth and she's okay. So all we have to do is get Bruce to kiss her and ...'

'No way!' yelled Bruce, hopping back indignantly. 'You blasted well kiss her!'

'But I'm not a handsome prince,' I pointed out reasonably.

'If it's just a bit of apple stuck in her mouth it doesn't matter who kisses her,' reasoned Bruce.

'We could get Prince Peanut to do it,' suggested Phredde.

I glanced over at the marquee. Prince Peanut was giggling with The Phaery Daffodil and she was feeding him little bits of moonblossom sorbet with her spoon.

'I think he's occupied,' I said. 'And anyway, you know what he's like! He'd expect to marry her, and then The Phaery Daffodil would get upset and go round capturing humans and making people pies again and ...' I looked pleadingly at Bruce. 'You have to help her!'

Bruce gulped. 'Can't I just shake hands with her instead?' he asked.

'Bruce!'

'Alright! Let's just ... look at her. Just to see if we can get the apple out some other way.'

'But you'll kiss her if we can't?' I insisted.

'Well, maybe,' said Bruce.

That seemed about as good an answer as we were going to get. I glanced around at the wedding party. Mum and Dad were with Phredde's and Bruce's parents doing these real old-time dances on the other side of the marquee, and no one seemed to be paying any attention to us at all.

'Okay,' I said, 'here's the plan. I'll go and grab a bowl of salad for the trolls.'

'Two bowls of salad,' said Phredde. 'We have to pay troll toll coming back too.'

'Good point,' I said. 'I'll grab two bowls of salad and meet you down on the yellow brick road. Okay?'

'Okay,' whispered Bruce. Not that there was any need to whisper — not with all the music and chattering and stuff, and anyway, no one was even *looking* at us. But it just seemed proper to whisper somehow.

I tiptoed off to grab the salad.

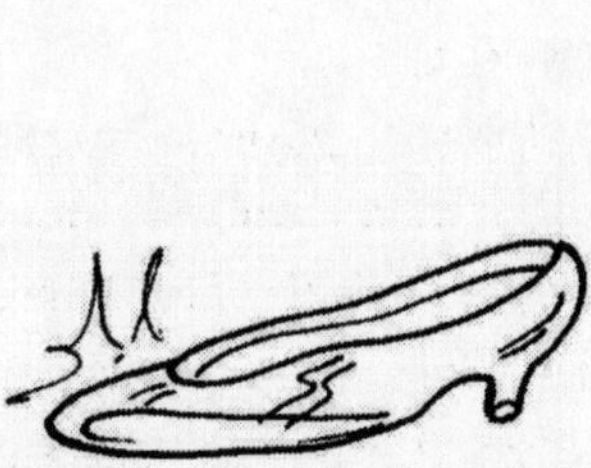

eighteen

Bruce Does a Brave Thing

The lollipop forest was all shadows and moonlight. (I had a feeling every night was moonlit in Phaeryland.) The yellow brick road glowed in the dimness, and the lollipops shone an eerie reddish purple through the trees.

'That way,' said Phredde, pointing through the forest.

'No, that way,' said Bruce.

'I think it's over there,' I said.

Well, anyway, to cut a *really* long story short, we went my way, then Phredde's way, then it turned out Bruce was right, and *eventually* (I learnt that word in spelling last term — I was the only kid except for Amelia who got it right first time) there was the glade. And there was Snow White too, on her bed or table or bier or whatever it was. (A bier isn't stuff you drink. I looked it up when *eventually* we got home.)

'Well, go on,' whispered Phredde. It was a bit spooky in that forest, to tell the truth. You felt you *had* to whisper. 'Kiss her!'

'No way!' said Bruce. 'You promised we'd investigate first!'

'I didn't promise!' whispered Phredde hotly. '*You* said ...'

'Sh ... shush up!' I ordered. (Like I've said, you can't use even sort of bad language in Phaeryland.) 'Phredde, you find a twig or something and we'll prise her mouth open.'

'Why?' asked Phredde.

'To see if there's any poisoned apple in there, of course!' I told her.

Phredde went off to pick up a twig, and Bruce and I walked (well, I walked and he hopped) over to the bier. It was even spookier than the forest. I mean, okay, we knew she was just asleep, but even so ...

I peered over her. 'I can't see any bit of apple,' I said.

Bruce shook his head. 'If you could see it Grumpy and the others would have seen it too.'

'Here,' said Phredde as she handed me the twig.

Well, this was *really* gruesome, but anyway, I sort of prised Snow White's mouth open and we peered in.

Lots of strong, white teeth (she must really be good with her toothbrush). One tongue, a bit furry, but after all she'd been asleep awhile. But no apple. I stepped back

'You'll have to kiss her,' I informed Bruce.

'And you'd better change back into a phaery prince too,' added Phredde.

'What!' yelled Bruce, so loudly that a bird in one of the lollipop trees woke up and began going *tweet, tweet, tweet*.

'Well, you have to be a prince, not a frog,' said Phredde reasonably.

Bruce appealed to me. 'I don't, do I?' he demanded.

I thought about it. To be really honest, I've always wondered what Bruce would look like if he weren't a frog.

'How about Phredde and I cover our eyes?' I suggested.

'You won't peek?' demanded Bruce suspiciously.

I crossed my fingers behind my back. 'You don't think we'd peek, do you?'

'Yes,' said Bruce.

Phredde sniffed. 'Of course we won't peek,' she said. 'Why would we want to?'

I uncrossed my fingers. After all, I hadn't lied. I just hadn't said anything when Phredde said ... well, you know what I'm saying.

Phredde covered her face with her hands. So did I.

PING! I opened my fingers a little just as Bruce bent over and ...

'Hey, what on earth is going on?' Snow White sat up and blinked indignantly at Bruce.

PING! Suddenly Bruce was a frog again.

'Did you kiss her? Did you kiss her?' demanded Phredde.

Snow White wiped her mouth. 'Of course he didn't kiss me,' she said.

'I shook her hand,' said Bruce. 'And look!' he pointed.

I looked. There on the ground was a computer mouse, small and grey and innocent-looking.

'Wow!' said Phredde. 'I bet that's a poisoned Apple Macintosh mouse! And when Bruce shook her hand he dislodged it!'

'And I know just who poisoned it,' said Snow White grimly. 'Help me up, kids! This means war!'

'Swords and knights and cannons and stuff?' I asked hopefully. 'Hey, I know some really good ninja moves! Maybe I could ...'

'No, corporate war!' said Snow White firmly, brushing a few dead leaves and cobwebs off her skirt. 'We're going to get that new program on the market pronto and totally undercut my stepmother's entire price range! Then we'll see whose magic mirror says they've got the best software on the market!'

She looked us up and down briefly. 'Well, thank you kids,' she said briskly. 'I really do appreciate this, but I have to get to work. But if you ever have any computer glitches, here's my email address.' She handed us each a card. 'Don't hesitate to let me know and I'll get one of my best people on to it immediately.'

'Er, thanks,' I said, putting the card into my pocket. I'd been sort of hoping for gold and jewels or something, but then Phredde can always magic gold and jewels up for me, and good computer advice could be *really* useful.

'Ciao!' said Snow White, and hurried off through the forest.

'Hey!' I called after her. 'Your seven partners are at the Phaery Queen's wedding. You want us to tell them where you are?'

'Tell them I want to see them in the boardroom! Pronto!' yelled Snow White, and disappeared into the gloom.

nineteen

A Bit of Old-time Dancing

So we went back to the wedding.

Mum and Dad were still dancing close together with this soppy look on their faces, and so were Phredde's and Bruce's parents. I sidled up to the seven short computer software engineers and whispered what had happened.

Grumpy's eyes brightened. 'Hot diggetty!' he yelled. 'Come on guys! Hi ho, hi ho, a-programming we'll go!'

They raced out of the marquee, past the elf musicians and the dancers.

'Ummm.'

I turned round. Mordred stood behind us, staring at Phredde. 'Ummm,' he said again.

'Hi,' said Phredde. She glanced at me, and winked. 'You want to dance?' she asked Mordred kindly.

Mordred blushed so red he looked like a prawn

kebab. 'Ummm,' he said happily, as Phredde hauled him off to the dance floor.

I looked at Bruce. There was something I needed to confess. 'Er, Bruce,' I said.

'Yes,' said Bruce, looking hungrily round the marquee lights. 'You know, the trouble with Phaeryland is that there are never any flies hanging round the roast meat! Or even any moths around the lights! Now, back home on a warm night like this there'd be blowies and a few mosquitoes ...'

'Look,' I said, 'I have to tell you something.'

'What?' asked Bruce.

'You know back in the forest, when you changed out of being a frog?'

'Yep,' said Bruce.

'I peeked,' I said.

'Oh,' said Bruce.

He was silent for a minute. Then he said, 'What did you think?'

'Oh,' I said carelessly. 'You look alright.'

We stared at each other for a minute. Then Bruce said, 'I don't suppose you want to dance?'

'Alright,' I said again.

So we did.

You know something? It was fun. I think Bruce even forgot about his embarrassing trousers and velvet shirt, and I sort of forgot he was a frog. I mean, he was just Bruce and we were friends and the music was cool, even if it was old fashioned and played by elves sitting cross legged on mushrooms.

'You know, Bruce,' I said.

'Yes,' said Bruce, gazing hopefully up into the night sky in case a leftover giant vampire mosquito was buzzing around.

'You know those ghouls that invaded your parents' castle?'

'Yeah,' said Bruce.

'Was it a really terrible battle?'

Bruce stared at me in the light from all the tapers and candles and stuff. 'Battle? There wasn't any battle.'

'But you said the ghouls invaded ... er, Bruce?'

'Yeah?' said Bruce.

'What *are* ghouls?'

'They're sort of grungy grey things. They eat dead bodies.'

'Oh, how horrible!' I said. 'Did they try to kill you all so they could gnaw your bones?'

'No, of course not,' said Bruce. 'Ghouls are really tiny. I mean, you just have to tread on them and they go *squish*, but there was this real plague of them and they kept dragging in these dead rats and mice and cockroaches and things and the whole place smelt *awful* no matter how much air freshener Mum used, and Mum said she couldn't stand it any more. So we left.'

'Oh,' I said. 'No battle?'

'Nope,' said Bruce.

'No swords and ... and knights on horseback and archers and ...'

'Nope,' said Bruce. 'We did get the pest exterminators in. But you know what ghouls are like.

Well, I suppose you don't. But you just get rid of one lot and another lot move in. Dad wanted to put up sticky traps but Mum said no, she'd had it with ghouls.'

'Oh,' I said again. 'I was thinking we could get the troll and Prince Peanut and The Phaery Daffodil and Mordred and the seven software engineers and everyone, and go and hunt the ghouls out, and reclaim your castle and ...'

'Well, actually,' said Bruce, 'Mum says she never wants to see the castle again. She'd rather have TV and wall-to-wall fitted carpet and a supermarket and a video bar down the road. And ... er,' he glanced at me, 'I really like living where we are now. But thanks anyway.'

'But wasn't she upset when you had to leave?' I asked.

Bruce gave a froggy shrug. 'Yeah, I suppose so. But she's really happy now. Hey, is that a fly on that prince's head?'

'No,' I said, 'it's a hat with a really small feather in it.'

'I'll just go and check it out,' said Bruce hungrily, and hopped off.

So I went and found Jessica the bogeyman (sorry, bogeyperson) and let her shout 'Boo!' at me a few hundred times while I finished off the moonlight and roses ice cream with pistachios and honeycomb.

And by that time the Phaery Queen's wedding was just about over ...

twenty

Back Home in the Castle

You know something? It was good to be home.

Our castle was just like we'd left it, except for a few bones Mark had left in the grand hallway. (They looked a bit like Persian kitten bones to me, but Mark said no, they were just Kentucky Fried Chicken, he and the boys had had a night out on the prowl.)

Your own home has a certain smell about it, doesn't it? Sort of an old-familiar-sofas-and-kitchen-cupboards-and-piranhas-in-the-moat sort of smell.

It was great to be back into routine too, and just do normal things, like make my bed and veg out with a book on the battlements and feed Mark's pet rat to the piranhas (no, I didn't really, I just told him I did) and wipe up the slobber from Dad's pet sloth and take the boa constrictor for a walk, or a slither anyway. It was even good to see Mark, but don't tell him I said so.

Gark (our butler)* made a special giant apple pie to welcome us back, and then we all watched this really cool ninja video (it was my choice) and then I went to bed.

'Night, Prune Face!' shouted Mark.

'Night, Dog's Breath!' I yelled back.

I snuggled up under my doona and counted the stars through the window. Sixty-two, sixty-three, sixty-four ...

'Goodnight, Pru,' said Dad from the door.

'Did you have a good time in Phaeryland?' asked Mum.

'Yeah, I suppose,' I said. 'How about you?'

'It was alright,' said Dad. 'Pity we missed the football though.'

'Don't *ever* mention glass slippers to me again!' said Mum. 'I'm still hobbling. Thank goodness for ugh boots. But, yes,' she glanced at Dad, 'it was fun.'

I waited till they'd both kissed me goodnight, then I said, 'Hey, Dad, Mum ...?'

'What?' said Dad a bit warily. 'Pru, if you're wondering what to give me for Christmas, a nice pair of socks is quite ...'

'No, nothing like that,' I said. (I'd decided what to give him for Christmas ages ago. It's sort of gigantic

*Who is a magicked magpie. See all the *Stories to Eat With* books.

and it's South American, but you'll have to wait to see what it is, just like Dad.)* 'I just thought — would you and Mum ever leave Australia?'

'What, for a holiday?' asked Dad.

'No, I mean for good.'

Dad looked at Mum. 'I suppose it's possible,' said Mum slowly. 'We wouldn't want to. But if ... oh, I don't know, if there was a war, or you or Mark were in danger here, or couldn't get a good education or something, well, yes, we might go. But it's not going to happen, Prudence, so don't worry about it.'

'I'm not worried,' I said. 'I was just thinking, that's all. It'd be pretty hard to leave your own country, wouldn't it? Even if it was Phaeryland?'

'Yeah,' said Dad gently. 'It'd be pretty hard.'

'It'd be hard to be different from everyone else too, wouldn't it?' I added. 'Even if it was sort of really cool different.'

'Yeah,' said Dad again.

They tiptoed out then (well, actually, they didn't, 'cause Mum's ugh boots were too big for her and went sort of *clomp, clomp, clomp*, especially with all the bandaids on her blisters, and Dad couldn't tiptoe if a horde of vampire ghosts were hunting him, but that's how parents are supposed to leave your room after they've kissed you goodnight).

And I tried to go to sleep.

I couldn't, though. My mind was too full of phaeries and trolls and handsome princes. And I

*See *Phredde and the Demon Duck of Doom* in 2002.

thought how different they all were from me, and then I thought that maybe all of us are different, in our own ways, and maybe none of us is really better or worse than anyone else, just different ...

And then I thought, fruitcakes! (Some of Phaeryland had rubbed off on me.) Don't be a soft little marshmallow, Prudence! Of *course* some people are better than others! I'm a heck of a lot better than Amelia, 'cause I don't boast and say what a genius I am (Amelia a genius? Huh!), and Bruce is much, *much* nicer than Prince Peanut, and Phredde is better than just about anyone else I know and I'm glad she's my best friend in the universe...

... and then I went to sleep.

PS Phredde got an invitation to Mordred's Temple of Gloom display at the end of term. She said it was really cool, but somehow I wasn't really interested. Now if it had been the Fangosaurus on display ... but that's another story ...*

*See *Phredde and the Demon Duck of Doom* in 2002.

STORIES TO EAT WITH A Banana

Meet Phredde, the phaery of grunge. She's tiny, ferocious and Pru's best friend. When Phredde's around, odd things can happen, but what with Pru's brother turning into a werewolf, and the teacher growing fangs, Pru needs all the help she can get . . .

Magic, fantasy, real life. Pru's beginning to wonder if there's really a difference.

A collection of hilarious stories to read when your brain wants something light to munch on — like a banana.

ISBN 0 207 19683 4

STORIES TO EAT WITH A Watermelon

When your teacher's a vampire, your brother's a werewolf, and your best friend's a fairy — sorry, phaery — what else can happen?

Well, girl-eating rose bushes for a start. And a frog named Bruce who refuses to help when you try to save Sleeping Beauty from the Prince. AND a dose of flu that gives all of the world's computers more than just a runny nose! When Pru and Phredde are around strange things can happen ... but at least you won't stop laughing!

Another hilarious collection of adventures about a phaery named Phredde.

ISBN 0 207 19738 5

STORIES TO EAT WITH A Blood Plum

There's a grey-fleshed zombie librarian tending her blood-starved books in the school library. There's a 5000-year-old Egyptian Mummy roaming the corridors ... not to mention giant slugs, the Snot Phaery, piranhas, a few werewolves and a giant sloth.

Can Phredde and Prudence escape?

Well, of course they can, you ding-dong.

But HOW do they escape? That's the question!

Another hilarious collection of terrifying stories about a phaery named Phredde.

ISBN 0 207 19771 7